TAKING IT SLOW

Doing Bad Things Book 3

JORDAN MARIE

Cover Art by Robin with Wicked By Design

Model: Terrence Cooper

Photographer: Wander Aguiar with Wander Aguiar Book Club

WARNING: This book contains sexual situations and other adult themes. Recommended for 18 and above.

❀ Created with Vellum

taking it SLOW

By:
Jordan Marie

A bottle of tequila

10 lime wedges

1 sexy blonde

Add in a crazy Vegas weekend

Lick and swallow

What do you get?

A recipe for disaster.

Last night I got married.

I think.

I was drunk off my ass, so it's not exactly crystal clear.

But I woke up with a ring on my finger, a marriage certificate, and a sneaking suspicion I'd had a wild wedding night.

Oh, and a bride who is long gone.

Apparently, what happens in Vegas doesn't always stay here.

Sometimes it takes off running.

Now I'm chasing after my runaway bride with divorce on my mind.

What could go wrong?

Besides everything.

DEDICATION

To my readers:
You inspire me every day. You make me someone who takes a chance, goes against the norm and embraces change. It takes courage, you give me that. You are part of the reason this world is so great and I am grateful to each of you.
Xoxo
J

1

FAITH

I whimper when the damn ping of my phone won't hush. I squint, opening one eye—and one eye only.

Sweet Jesus on a turnip truck, I drank way too much last night. I warned Hope I didn't do weddings. I hate them. She was in Vegas, and everyone knows you do the deed at a quicky drive-thru chapel somewhere and get it done—if you are ever crazy enough to say "I do."

I won't... ever.

Slowly the room begins to come into a focus... it's a blurry focus, but still.

The first thing I notice is everything hurts.

Even my hair.

Definitely had too much to drink. The second thing I notice is I'm not in my one-room apartment, lying on my broken-down, never comfortable, probably ruining my back forever, futon.

I'm in a bed. A *really* soft bed. I'm also in what appears to be a very fancy room. A room with entirely too much sunshine coming in through the windows. My gaze immediately goes to the open glass doors that lead out to a balcony. When I look around I can see I'm not only in a strange hotel room, I'm in one that costs bank.

Lots of bank.

Then, I just happen to notice the crumpled wedding dress on the concrete floor of the balcony.

That's when panic begins, as memories flood through my mind.

Memories of the night before.

Of course, it might not be the crumpled dress that brings those back quite as much as the huge leg—*not that leg*—wrapped over mine, the arm currently wrapped across my stomach and the third leg—*yes, that "leg"*—pushing against my ass.

I look down at the milk chocolate beast of an arm and I swear the female bits between my legs tingle as memories of the night before flood through me. Memories of... *Titan*. I have the strongest urge to wiggle against the semi-aroused cock pressing against my ass, but I don't. I hold myself really still.

Because I'm in the middle of the biggest panic attack ever.

I can't remember all of what I did last night. It's a blur of devil's juice, eating the worm—disgusting, by the way, and I may never drink tequila again—and sex... so much sex.

Sex everywhere. Bed, floor, shower, closet—don't ask—and against the wall. Sex against the floor-to-ceiling window with my ass mooning the strip, but... sex on that balcony after I was stripped of my wedding dress is the one that sticks in my mind. Sex where I hung over the concrete balcony screaming, *"Fuck me, harder, Big Daddy,"* while Titan did indeed fuck me harder for everyone and anyone to see. There are other balconies close by. I can't be entirely sure who saw us... or who we may have scarred forever.

Because, let's face it, sex in real life is never like the porn movies.

I slide out of the bed an inch at a time—panic making my heart slam against my chest so loud I want to cry, because my head hurts like hell. Titan grumbles but flops over on his back, still asleep. I stand there looking down at him and I can't move.

He's that beautiful.

His arms are slung out on each side, his head turned to the side, his well-trimmed goatee and beautiful, thick lips making my knees weak. The sheet is tangled in his feet and his dick is obviously alert, even if the rest of him isn't.

The sight of his dick makes me glad I was drunk last night.

Lord have mercy on me, a poor sinner girl... He's huge. I take a step toward it before I can stop myself. It's bobbing up in the air like it's nodding at me. It's wide, as in—thick as hell. How many women has this man sent running from the room in fear—*that kind of thick*. I've seen a few dicks—I'm not a whore or anything —*not counting last night*—but I have, and this one is in a class all by itself. And he's long. I don't have a tape measure on hand, and I wouldn't risk waking Titan up for it, but this man could be the pink unicorn of dicks. He could actually be a foot long. He might not be, but it would not surprise me. I back away when Titan grunts in his sleep. Each step I take hurts, only adding credence to Titan's dick. Damn, I might not walk right for a month.

I run bare-ass naked to the balcony. It's early, the sun is shining, but the Vegas heat hasn't raised its evil head yet. I'm definitely going to have to soak my poor abused body soon, however. I can feel where Titan has drilled—*so to speak*—with each step. I grab the wedding dress and step into it, trying to remain bent over so I cover my body. I might not have been shy last night in my tequila haze, but I don't have that luxury today. I shove my hands through the dress, rising up so I can zip it—when I hear a throat clearing. I look behind me and see a man standing on a balcony behind me, grinning.

He's older, as in probably Uncle Jansen's age, and he's wearing a cowboy hat. He's sexy, but not my style.

"Morning," he smirks, his Texan accent strong.

I give him a tight smile over my shoulder and then reach behind me to zip up the dress and hide my ass from the guy—even if it is a little too late. Walking back into the room, I look around for my shoes. I see some empty condom wrappers—*thank you Jesus!* I also see an empty bottle of tequila and Titan's clothes.

Titan Marsh... pro football player, a hell of a good time in bed, and ... *my husband.*

That last part makes me cringe. I don't want a husband. He didn't want a wife. We discussed that numerous times while drinking tequila and gambling the night away. How we ended up in that all-night Elvis wedding chapel, I don't remember exactly. But I clearly remember saying "I do" and twirling my hips like Elvis when he proclaimed us husband and wife. I also remember turning to Titan and demanding—in my best Meg Ryan voice—to take me to bed or lose me forever.

He did take me to bed, but he didn't get the whole Top Gun reference. I get the feeling Titan isn't a big movie buff.

I look around for a few more minutes and pick up my veil, looking at the white converse tennis shoes and frowning. I wore tennis shoes to my wedding?

Whatever.

I put them on and lace them up quickly. Just as I'm heading out the door, I find a blue flowered garter. It's on the entry table. I pick it up and start to stuff it into my pocket, but the dress doesn't have pockets.

I look back at Titan and then down to the gold band on my hand. I walk back toward him, still feeling him between my legs with each step I make. I clutch the garter tightly in my hand. As I look down at the sleeping man, with the dick that apparently never sleeps, I only know one thing. *I don't want to be married.*

He's damn good in bed, though.

Decision made, I toss my garter toward his dick. It snags on the wide head, and lands at an angle. Titan's hand comes down and he cups his balls before scratching them. I watch, my mouth falling open and my eyes widening in shock.

When the garter decides to fall down the long shaft of his dick I have to fight back a giggle. Then I hightail it out of the room. I don't stop to think, I don't stop to take in the strange stares I'm getting from the people in the elevator or in the lobby. I head straight for the door.

2

TITAN

I stretch and groan as I feel my back make a popping noise. Years of football are slowly catching up with me. I know I don't have many good years left in me. That's one reason I'm making the life choices I'm making—and I hate every fucking one of them. The life of a pro-baller is short for the most part and I was a stupid fuck and didn't plan for the future.

I move my neck back and forth and as it snaps and pops I begin to feel a little more human. I've got a fuck of a hangover. I don't remember much of last night. Just that I left Aden's wedding with a hot little blonde... She's obviously not here this morning, though. Too bad. I could have used a good workout before I load up and head back to Cali. I reach down to rub my balls, a silent apology, because they're hurting this morning. I frown when I feel lace material against my hand. I sit up and notice there's.... *a garter?* It's laying against my balls, my dick sticking up from the center of it.

I don't remember the chick from last night wearing garters... but she had on this sweet little dress that clung to her luscious ass, so it's possible, I guess. I pull the garter off, wadding it up in my hand.

Whatever.

She's gone and I need to get rolling too.

I stand up, stretching the kinks in my back. Yeah, I'm definitely getting too damn old for this shit. I look at the garter, and then throw it in the trash. It seems to stare back at me—mocking me. For some weird reason, I pick it up and toss it back on the bed.

In the shower, I relax into the hot spray, my eyes closed. I smell like lemons. Never really liked that fucking smell before, but yet it reminds me of Faith... *Faith Lucas*. That's her name. The longer I'm awake the more the memory of her begins to come back. Gorgeous bod, definitely a ten, and that ass is an ass to make men beg. I can't really remember what we did last night... but my balls are sore, so I'm hoping that means it was fucking good.

I reach over to the bottle of body wash and grow completely still. The bottle is black, my hand the same brown it's always been, but the gold band on my finger...

Now that's definitely new.

I drop the bottle like it's hot, ignoring the way it crashes against the tile. I stomp out, not caring water is going everywhere, not caring I don't have a towel. I trace my steps, and then look in the main bedroom. There's nothing really out of place there. Condom wrappers and an empty bottle of Patron... I'd pat myself on the back if I wasn't sporting a damn ring on my finger.

I walk through the rest of the giant room. The small sofa in front of the television grabs my attention. More importantly, the manila envelope on the sofa grabs my attention.

I all but rip it open and what I find has me falling back on my ass. The couch scoots a good foot with my weight, but I don't care. All I can think about are the two large words at the top of the paper I'm holding.

Marriage... Certificate...

Fuck.

3

FAITH

"What do you mean you've left Vegas?" Hope asks, and I hear *that* voice.

I know that voice.

That's the voice that she gets whenever she's about to go into big sister mode. The voice she always gets when she wants to begin her *Faith-you-can't-go-through-life-and-never-grow-up* speech. I hate that speech. In fact, today is too pretty to hear it.

"Just what I said. I got tired of Vegas. I've decided to move on."

"Tired... decided to move on..."

"That's what I said," I repeat. "Listen, Sis, I got to go." I'm preparing to shut her down. I look out at the totally empty road—except for me and my Jeep—and shrug. "Traffic is really starting to pick up. I need to concentrate on the road."

"Faith... Sis, Titan was just here and... He's looking for you."

I capture the corner of my lip between my teeth and worry it back and forth while I think about that. I kind of knew Titan would be looking for me... I did. It didn't occur to me he'd go to my sister and Aden—mostly because it is their honeymoon. I thought maybe he'd ask White. I frown because I'm not happy with him. It feels like he's telling on me to my sister—which kind of pisses me off.

"Titan? That's interesting," I answer, trying to come off like I don't have a care in the world—which is really what my sisters expect. I'm the blond airhead of the family, bouncing from place to place with no direction or ambition. I play my part well... too well. "Did he say what he wanted?"

"No... but Faith, he seemed angry."

"That's strange and I have no idea why. You have my number. You can give it to him. Listen, Sis, I really have to go. Traffic is crazy. Enjoy your honeymoon! Talk to you soon."

I hang up before she can answer me. Then, to be safe, I switch the phone on silent and toss it in the back seat.

Titan is a complication that I can't wrap my head around right now. I'm running. My sisters think I've spent my whole life running, floating around like a butterfly. I let them think that. The truth is much more depressing.

I keep moving because I just don't belong anywhere.

Titan is a complication I don't need. A wild, careless night of sex should be kept in the bucket list. I checked it off and it's done. I look down at the ring on my finger and get more than a little nauseous.

Okay, a night of sex probably shouldn't be preceded with a marriage ceremony. That was a mistake. I should never drink tequila when I'm upset. I never wanted marriage. My parents were a shining example of why the words "I do" should never be uttered.

And why I planned never to utter them...

Especially after my last relationship.

I pull up to a stop sign. I'm on a back road in the middle of nowhere. I have my suitcase in the back—with my phone—and I do not have a plan. I just know I need a fresh start.

Do I go left or right? I pull out a penny from my ashtray, which has been converted into a change holder. Then I flip it up in the air. I don't bother catching it, I suck at that. Heads will be right;

tails will be left. The penny lands on the dash, rolling and sliding, but spins to a stop.

I smile. Tails it is! It feels good. I keep the penny handy.

I'm sure there are more turns ahead.

4

TITAN

"You got married?"

"You don't have to shout, Cora. I'm not deaf."

"No, just stupid. Who the fuck did you marry?"

"A sister... of a friend," I answer, having no other words. Besides, that sounds better than *some blonde I fucked all night*.

"You're engaged!"

"Well, not officially," I grumble.

"Fuck officially! You're all but engaged. What do you think you're doing? This could ruin everything!"

"Meyers could still offer me the position, even if I don't marry his daughter," I growl. I haven't been happy with the decisions I'm making anyways. Sure, Jacey is a sweet girl. I like her, she likes me. I never wanted marriage, though. I didn't go into this thinking of it as a marriage; it was more of a contract. I marry Jacey, I get my shot at being general manager of the Turnpikes. Jacey gets her trust fund from her father completely and can use the money to open up the art gallery her father thinks is a waste of time.

We both win out of the deal and we have reasonable chemistry together... I guess... We've gone on a few dates. Shared a few kisses... okay, I have no fucking idea if we have any chemistry. I don't think of her like that, and I'm pretty sure she doesn't me either. In fact, I get the impression the woman could care less about my dick. It's a new feeling for me, but I didn't care. We agreed we go into this marriage with the goal of getting what we want and staying out of each other's ways. What Daddy Meyer doesn't know won't hurt either of us.

That was the plan... *Until Faith.*

"You have to divorce her, Titan. There's no other way."

Cora takes being my agent seriously. Right now she's annoying the shit out of me, however.

"Yeah, well, there's just one little problem with that," I growl, rubbing the back of my neck.

"What?"

"I can't find her."

"You. Can't. *Find her?*" And this time she screams those last two words out so loud that I have to hold the phone away from my ear.

"Woman, you're starting to piss me off. I'm not one of your lapdogs that sits and rolls over at your command," I growl.

"Well, that's obvious, Titan. If you were, you would have already been GM of the Turnpikes and you and I would be sitting pretty with your huge bonus and my fat commission."

I bring my hand down to my lap and tighten it into a fist, frustrated at Cora, for sure—but more so at myself. She's not saying anything I haven't thought myself since getting out of bed this morning. I look down at the wedding ring on my finger, still not quite processing what I've done and what a fucked-up mess this has all become.

"I'll handle it," I tell Cora, but I have no idea what I'm going to do.

"You better. I don't need to remind you that you need this money as much as I do," she growls, slamming the phone down.

She's right too. I do need the money. When I said I hadn't planned for my future I wasn't shitting. My accounts aren't gone yet, but they're fucking low and I'm looking at getting cut from the roster for the next season. I need this position. If I don't get it,

I'm going to end up some sad color commentator on a second-rate network—and that's if I even get that kind of offer. Those usually go to the golden boys. Whose skin is pale—or at least lighter than mine, who are pretty in the face and have charm. None of that is me.

Never has been and never will be.

I drop the phone, contemplating my next move. Hope was zero help. That leaves only one... White and that crazy, fucked-up family of his. They're all probably still around the hotel somewhere.

I find that damn blonde, I'm going to smack her ass for making me chase her down.

I ignore the way that thought makes my dick happy. He's never getting back inside of her.

And that news doesn't make either me or my dick happy.

5

FAITH

I thought Colorado would be more exciting. I've been here for a week and so far, the only thing exciting I've found... *Yeah... I got nothing.*

When I left the hotel room that morning, I drove until I got tired and that ended me here—Buck-Stop, Colorado. I can't tell you how I ended up here, but I'm pretty sure the penny I used was stuck on tails, because my trip here was a series of left turns.

I never knew Buck-Stop existed and near as I can tell, it's not on the map, which is good when you're in the hot water I'm in. I'm not just talking about that sexy Godiva dark chocolate man that I left in Vegas, either. Although, I guess that's the one I keep looking over my shoulder for. I have other things influencing my flight though. I have an ex-boyfriend that's been calling. One I definitely do *not* want to hear from. I didn't have a great time in that relationship and with one hit from him, I was done. I left him with my knee planted in his balls and slammed the door while he was rolling on the floor. Hearing from him is bad juju. Add in the fact that my sister Hope has called me constantly. She's called so much I'm pretty sure she's been *laying into* me more than she's *laying* her husband. Which is bad, since technically she's still on her honeymoon.

All that adds up to the reason I "accidentally" dropped my phone in a motel's bathroom. The silence has been bliss.

I got a job at a gas station. I got to say I liked dealing blackjack in Vegas much better—but then, that got me into more trouble than I care to remember. I'm not planning on staying here forever. *I can't.*

"Hey, Girl, your new uniform came in this morning. Go put it on and don't drag your feet. We've got a busy schedule today," my new boss informs me while walking out of his office.

He knows my name, but he constantly calls me "Girl." It's beyond annoying and I might dream of knocking him over the head with a tire iron in my spare time. He deposits a small paper bag on the counter. I look at it and my eyes nearly bulge out of my head. I could barely fit a sandwich in there, let alone a uniform.

I pull out... *a bikini.*

"You have got to be shitting me," I respond, holding up the skimpiest white bikini I have ever seen in my life. The top will barely cover my boobs and it's studded. There's literally silver studs all over it, making it shiny and glittery as hell. The bottom will mostly cover my ass, so I guess I should be glad it's not thong style.

"You got a problem?"

"You expect me to wear a bikini in a gas station? Have you seen this place, Joe? I'll be covered in oil by the end of the day. And why do I need to wear a bikini? I stand behind a counter all day."

"You'll be pumping gas," he responds. He sounds like he thinks I'm just being plain stupid not knowing what's expected of me.

See, there are no 7/11s or regular Chevron or Shell stations in Buck-Stop. There's Joe's. Joe's is a gas station that looks like it stepped out of a 1970s sitcom. It has the old style 1980s pumps and he still literally has the black tube a car drives over that makes a bell ring when someone pulls up outside for gas. The inside doesn't have a store. It has snacks, one freezer housing sodas—chest type, no fancy pop machine at Joe's—and car supplies like oil, brake fluid, windshield washing fluid, antifreeze and so on.

Still, he pays in cash, which is nice, because I've been using my credit card to the point that I think I can hear it screaming every time they swipe it. I just never planned on wearing a bikini.

"You want me to pump gas wearing a bikini? *Outside?*"

"You can't very well pump gas inside, now can you? You going to talk my head off all day or go put your uniform on?"

"It's a bikini, not a uniform," I argue, frowning.

"Are we going to have a problem? I could have hired other people, you know, Girl. You either do it or get out, but don't expect me to pay you for today because you haven't done anything to earn me one dime."

"You do realize we are in Colorado, right? That the weather is freaking cold?"

"It's not like you'll be out there all day. You'll have breaks to come inside. Make up your mind. You're starting to wear on my nerves," he grumbles.

For a minute I'm torn. I really want to tell him to go fuck himself. But my bank account needs to moderately recover before I can hop back on the road and play left or right turn into the next state. So instead, I sigh. Then I take the bikini and head to the back office.

I'm changing the damn penny next time. Clearly I should have been turning right when leaving Vegas behind.

6

TITAN

Getting a call from a private investigator at two in the morning informing you that your *wife* is somewhere in Colorado is not exactly what every man dreams of, I'm sure. It sure as fuck isn't what I wanted. After a week of hearing nothing from her, I can admit I was starting to panic. I have plans and my actions kind of derailed them. They weren't plans I'm necessarily proud of and I've been thinking twice about them—actually a lot more than twice. But they were plans, and either way I moved forward I didn't need to do it with a ring on my damn finger. A ring I'm still wearing. I like to look down at it and remind myself that I'm an idiot.

An idiot that should never drink Patron.

I let the information lay for a bit. By my calculations, my runaway bride will have been in Colorado for over two weeks. I had hoped that by now she would have reached out to me. That hasn't been the case and I'm starting to worry. Cora, on the other hand, is trying to go ballistic on me. With each day that passes, I'm thinking of saying screw it on the Turnpike's general manager position. If I do that, I'm pretty sure I'll have to find another agent.

Finding Buck-Stop Colorado wasn't as easy as you would think. The damn place isn't on the freaking map. Apparently it's a *self-proclaimed* city that broke away from a larger one. The larger one had a huge population of eight hundred—insert sarcasm here. Buck-Stop has a recorded population of three hundred. Apparently three hundred and one, since Faith has decided to take up residence.

I drove for six hours straight and then crashed at a dive hotel off the interstate before starting back on the road at six this morning. It is now two in the afternoon, which means I've been on the road a fuck of a long time. I'm hungry, my car is running on fumes and there's a picture of a blonde with a killer ass in my head, and with every mile I change from thinking about spanking her raw, to throttling her.

I should have stopped to eat a while back, because I'm getting the feeling there will be nothing in Buck-Stop. Up ahead I see a garage with a sign that says "Joe's." I'm hoping they at least sell gas, or I could be stranded here. That wouldn't be healthy for me or for Faith at this point.

Joe's must be the only damn station around because there's a line. I'm talking there's at least a row of ten cars in front of me. Jesus. I pull up behind a beat-up old Ford pickup and wait. I cut off the car and roll the windows down to conserve gas. The damn warning light with the little pump came on about ten miles back. I don't know how much more I have before it goes completely empty. I turn the radio off and once again find myself staring at the ring on my finger.

"That's it, baby. Clean that windshield," I hear a man shout out.

"You tell her, Earl," another says.

"If I knew old Joe had this kind of service, I never would have moved out of the city."

"You and me both," another says.

I think it's pretty clear this town might be completely insane. I blot it out and breathe a sigh of relief when I can move up. I can't tell you how long I stayed in line, but I know it has to be around twenty or thirty minutes. Finally, there are only two cars in front of me. I've never seen anything like it. I have to wonder if there's a storm in the forecast and people are panicking, wanting to make sure their tanks are filled. That's when I see exactly what is causing all of the uproar.

I can't see great, because there's a truck between us. But there's a woman in a fucking bikini with her ass stuck out checking the air in a tire. I can't see her face, but I'm getting a damn good view of her ass. She's got sexy legs. Not long, but tanned and gorgeous. She's wearing heels too. It's the most ridiculous thing I've ever seen, considering this is a gas station in fucking Colorado.

I have to admit I enjoy the view, however. That barely-there white bikini rises up against some fucking luscious ass cheeks. One of them has a birthmark on it. It's a cute little thing. I can't see it really good and sadly, the woman moves before I can see it better.

"I need to you check my antifreeze too, girl. Seems like my old motor has been running pretty damn hot today," the man says.

"You can say that again, Leroy." The guy in front of me laughs, elbowing the other guy as the girl walks around the truck. They block her from me for the most part, which is damn sad—but I figure my time is coming. Whoever the owner of this place is, he's a fucking genius. Already, I see ten cars behind me and I'd swear two of those were in front of me when I got here.

"I swear, Leroy, that's one big engine you have there."

"I can rev it up for you, darlin', if you want."

"I dare you," the little flirt laughs.

I never seen anything move as fast as Leroy does in that moment. He runs to his vehicle like the hounds of hell are nipping at his feet. Then he starts up the ratty-ass sounding truck and guns the gas a couple of times before shutting it off.

"Oh my goodness," she cries, as if she's almost in the throes of an orgasm. "I just can't get over how *big* and *powerful* it is."

I'm almost laughing my ass off, when recognition slams into me.

I know that voice—*as in I know it biblically*.

Fucking hell... that's my *wife* up there flirting with those damn men and causing a traffic jam as thick as LA rush hour.

My decision is made.

I'm going to throttle her.

7

FAITH

"Oh my goodness," I tell Leroy, making sure I sound like I'm way *too* excited. "I just can't get over how *big* and *powerful* it is."

I'm going to hell. I know it. Shit, at this point I'm probably going to drive the bus. When Joe started this a week ago, I thought about quitting. There was one fringe benefit to freezing my ass off, however, that I didn't count on.

I am freaking rolling in the tips. When I say that, I mean that today starts week two. Last week I made two hundred and fifty dollars cash from Joe for five days. I made over a thousand in tips. Over three hundred of that came from old Leroy himself. Today he's been here three times already and I've pocketed well over two hundred from him alone. I think that means week two is shaping up to beat last week. At this rate, I'll have money in the bank by the time I leave Buck-Stop behind.

That's if I don't die from the flu. I'm freezing. The only saving grace that I have is that with the bikini top covered in studs and sparkly like it is, you can't tell my nipples are about to poke through the damn fabric.

"Damn, Faith, I forgot. I'm going to need you to fill up the wiper fluid too," Leroy says.

"Didn't I just fill that up for you yesterday, Leroy?"

"What can I say, baby? I like to make things wet," he says and I giggle—when I want to roll my eyes.

"You're so bad," I laugh, wondering if they can tell how fake it is. I pick up the jug of wiper fluid that I keep stacked up by the pump—I stacked thirty bottles here before the place opened this morning and after this one there will only be five left. Men are so damn predictable. Then I turn around—giving them the view they want, which is my ass bent over as I lean over their truck to get to the wiper fluid thing-a-ma-du-ma-fla-jit. I could reach it without bending over, but my tips are nowhere as good.

"You take good care of me, Faith."

"You might want to get your tank checked, Leroy. It's completely empty. I don't understand it," I tell him, playing stupid.

"You should let me take you away from all of this, Faith. Let me take care of you," he says, and he's moved in close behind me.

That's nothing new. He's been working up the courage to get bolder and bolder. Leroy is older. Probably in his mid-fifties. He's not bad looking for his age, but even if I hadn't sworn off men until the next century—totally not my type. I glance at the wedding ring I'm wearing and frown. Come to think of it, I don't really have a good track record with "my type."

I finish pouring in the fluid when old Leroy gets up his nerve and slaps his hand on my right ass cheek. It stings and I cry out in surprise. He then proceeds to squeeze it tightly. I'm about to knee him in the balls when I hear a voice I honestly didn't want to hear again.

"Old man, if you want to keep that hand you better get it off my woman's ass."

Titan.

Crap. I bite down on my lip and try to get up my courage and then carefully turn around with a smile on my face, like I don't have a care in the world.

"Hi, Big Daddy."

8

TITAN

I'm pissed as hell as I storm around the vehicles to get to the woman who has been doing nothing but giving me a headache, haunting my dreams, and generally making my life a living hell the last few weeks. I'm all set to light into her, but one thing stops me.

I look down and see that damn man's hand on her. He's got his hand on her ass. His fingers are stretched across one juicy cheek and digging in enough that you can see the outline of his fingers as they bite into her soft skin. His hand looks wrong on her. It's older, weathered and has tinges of oil here and there. That's not it. That's not what I don't like about it. What I don't like most about it is that it's not mine. That makes zero sense, but it's definitely true.

Then, the damn woman turns around as pretty as you please, leans back against the old truck like she doesn't have a care in the world, and taunts me.

"Hi, Big Daddy."

Memories of our night in Vegas

Even with her turned around, the stupid ass *Leroy* still has his hand on her ass.

"For real, man. Take your fucking hand off my wife's ass," I warn him, ignoring Faith right now.

"Wife?" Leroy mumbles. "You married to this guy, Faith?"

"That fucking ring on her finger tell you anything, asshole?" I answer. Faith looks down at her hand, frowning.

"There's no call for you to get pissed here, son."

"This is not pissed. This is mildly upset. You don't take your hand off Faith's ass, you will see pissed then."

"I don't want any trouble. Didn't know the little lady was married."

"There won't be trouble... If you *move* your fucking hand."

Leroy seems to size me up and then he holds his hands up like that should make me happy. *It doesn't.* Although at this point I'm more pissed at Faith than anything—*or anyone*—else.

"If it was my woman, I wouldn't be letting her work for old Joe. I sure wouldn't be letting her do anything dressed like she is."

"Damn woman didn't stay where I put her."

"They can be contrary like that," Leroy agrees, relaxing.

"The *woman,* as you so delicately put it, has a brain of her own," Faith huffs, obviously offended.

I let my eyes rake over her, taking in her body from head to toe. She's better than my tequila-soaked brain remembered. All tits, ass, and legs, and all of it better than good. Her face, though, it's fucking extraordinary. Delicate, in a way you want to admire it, caress... *Own it.* Her eyes are pools that seem to glitter and if a man's not careful he could drown in them. Hell, even her eyebrows are something. Perfectly formed and they have a way of curving when she's annoyed—which she is most definitely at this moment—that made my dick sit up and take notice.

"Don't look like it," I tell her, and as if on cue there goes them damn eyebrows. Her face colors and those blue pools narrow at me. For some damn reason, I fight a smile.

"What are you saying?"

"Any woman with a brain wouldn't be prancing her ass in the cold wind of Colorado like you are," I answer her, point blank.

"It's my uniform," she growls and she leans into me. As she does so I worry her damn tits are going to fall out of her bikini top.

"It's a fucking bikini, *wife*."

"It's the uniform Joe gave me to wear, *Big Daddy*."

"Then I'll be dealing with *Joe* next."

"Huh?"

"Get your shit together. Been chasing your ass for weeks. Got stuff to do."

"Got stuff to do?"

"That's what I said." Any other time this back and forth might be mildly amusing. Right now, it's annoying. Probably a mixture of things beginning and ending with Faith.

"Then might I suggest you go do them and leave me alone. I'm happy here."

"Can't do that, considering we're married now."

"Wait, how long you been married?" Leroy asks, and I let out a breath which sounds more like a rumbling growl. I thought he left. Faith doesn't realize it just yet, but I'm getting very close to the edge of my control.

"Almost a month," I answer him, my look and tone warning him I could snap him like a damn stick.

"One day," Faith answers obstinately. I find myself rubbing above my eye, irritation trying to bring on a headache and that headache has my "wife's" name on it.

"One day?"

"We were married in Vegas, Leroy, in a drunken haze of tequila."

"You forgot the sex, *wife*."

"I didn't forget. I just didn't want to bring it up, *Big Daddy*."

I'm going to spank her ass.

"No need to be embarrassed now," I mock her. Since she's been gone, I've remembered some of our *wedding* night and one of the best memories is the way she screamed and begged for me out on the balcony.

"Are you sure?" she asks. There's something in her question that makes me curious.

"Definitely," I tell her—mostly because I don't like the idea of Faith being ashamed of anything we did together, even if the alcohol was to blame.

"Whatever. Can you leave? Joe's going to get tired of me standing around and I need to earn money."

"If you were my woman, you wouldn't need to worry about money, Faith," Leroy says, making his ass known again. I really need to squash that asshole.

"Aw, Leroy, you're such a sweetie. And I want you to know your tips have helped me greatly. I almost have enough saved up."

"What are you saving for, darlin'?"

"A divorce."

"Well now, you don't say. How much do you need for this divorce?"

"You're shitting me right now," I growl, interrupting their conversation.

Faith looks up at me, blinking her eyes and trying to look as innocent as the day she was born.

Why do I get the feeling she's never been innocent in her life?

9

FAITH

He looks good.

I don't especially want to notice that, but I do. He looks really good—even with his eyes boring holes into me and his face looking like he wants to choke me. Of course he'll have to get in line. I apparently have that effect on men.

"I need another thousand," I sigh sadly, smiling at old Leroy.

"A thousand?" Titan asks, outrage—or maybe disbelief—laced through his voice.

"Divorce ain't cheap, Big Daddy." I smile, giving my best *"I'm innocent"* face.

"Why are you divorcing him, sweet cheeks?"

I blink at Leroy's new pet name. Since he's had his hand on my cheeks—as it were—I probably should be flattered.

"I'd be interested in hearing that since you got my ass drunk to get me to the altar."

"I what?" I can't believe he said that. I mean, I guess I shouldn't be, but I am.

"Didn't stutter, *sweet cheeks*."

"I did not get you drunk. You got me drunk."

"Bullshit."

"It's true!" And it mostly is. He did buy the bottle of Patron and convince me we had to do shots every time we lost at blackjack. It should be said that Titan is a horrible blackjack player, and I'm worse—*especially when getting drunk.*

"Got to say, buddy. I'm buying little Faith's version here a lot more than yours."

"Stay out of this, old man."

"I might be old, but I'm not stupid."

"You'll excuse me if I'm not buying that. You're the asshole who had his hands on my wife's ass. That's pretty fucking stupid."

"Doesn't sound like Faith is planning on staying your wife. I think that'd make her and her gorgeous ass fair game. Is this the guy Joe mentioned has been calling and bothering you, Faith?"

"Awe, Leroy. You think I have a gorgeous ass?" I ask him, ignoring his question about the guy aggravating me. My ex tracked me down here—somehow. He hasn't called the last few days though, so I'm hoping that means he has finally got the message that I'm done with him.

"That you do, darlin'. Prettier than the sunrise over the Rockies."

"You are just a sweet talker, aren't you?" I giggle. Leroy is a letch, but he is a cute letch and mostly harmless. Plus, I think any woman would agree that it's always nice to be told you have a gorgeous ass.

"Just stating the truth."

"Man, you're pushing me," Titan says and, gee, he sounds almost... *jealous.* I decide to block that out. I think I liked it, which is crazy—so I decide to block that fact out too. I don't need to like anything about Titan.

"I just look at Faith here and see that a man would snatch that up in a hot minute."

"I think this ring on my hand says I did, *Leroy.* If you don't mind, I need to have a conversation with my wife. And man, it's a conversation that don't need to include you."

"But I think you're wrong. The little lady here doesn't exactly seem happy to be around you. You don't seem exactly happy to be married to her."

"He does have a point, Big Daddy," I add helpfully. To which I swear I can see a vein thump in agitation above Titan's left eye. It's cute and right away I have to wonder if I can make his eye twitch. "You're very wise, Leroy," I praise him—trying my best not to giggle at Titan's groan of frustration.

Then Titan does something I wasn't expecting. He has a black sports jacket over a purple silk button-up. He takes it off and hangs it over my shoulders. It swallows me and lays heavy on my arms. But it's soft, it smells like Titan—which is to say, it smells really, *really* freaking good. It's also really warm, almost hot and feels heavenly. So I let it stay there.

He was being nice, it's the least I can do.

"Thank you, darlin'," Leroy continues. "Now, as I was saying, don't matter that Faith came with a nail for your coffin in the shape of a ring—"

"Uh... gee, Leroy—"

"You still marry her, for a chance to get in her pussy."

And there it is.

Suddenly ol' letch Leroy is starting to get on my nerves. I always did have horrible taste in men. Maybe he's not so harmless after all.

"Leroy—" I try to interject.

"And a real man will not risk getting drunk so his dick won't perform when he gets near her pussy," Leroy goes on, determined to get his point across. I have to admit once again he does have a wise point—in a gross, *I might be a pervert and not harmless* kind of way. "So I don't buy your story." Leroy finishes up his thoughts, and I really hope he's finished now. I'm not sure I want to hear more of Leroy's facts of life—even if he does think I have a gorgeous ass.

That gorgeous ass part needed repeated again, really.

"You keep talking about my wife's pussy and you and I got

problems, Jack," Titan answers, and his voice sounds all... *rumbly* and I'm thinking that doesn't mean wine and roses for Leroy.

"Okay, so maybe we should break this up," I announce when another car drives off. "Joe's going to be upset when he comes back out if he sees I'm not working," I tell them, but both men are ignoring me.

Isn't that special.

"I would have to believe that Faith would have to be drunk to marry your *kind,* though," Leroy says and damn it, not only is Leroy a pervert, what he just said—and the way he said it—makes it pretty clear he's a racist pervert.

I really don't have good judgment when it comes to men.

"You fucking jerk. If you think you can insult me, man, you're going to have to come up with a better game than that. I've been around the best of you spewing that—"

"Okay fine!" I yell, getting in between the two men. This is as close as I've seen Titan come to losing control. I don't think it'd be good if he wipes the floor with Leroy—even if he deserves it. I'd probably feel guilty and have to bail him out of jail. That would put a serious dent in my money supplies. So it's definitely time to defuse the situation. "He's right, Leroy. I got him drunk."

"You what?" Leroy asks, clearly not believing me, and I feel Titan's anger still boiling, even if I have my back turned to him. That might not be wise, but I figure if I'm standing in front of Titan and facing Leroy, Titan can't kill Leroy—thus ending up in jail and making me spend my money on bail.

"I got him drunk. I fell victim to the lust of the trouser snake."

"The trouser snake?"

That question comes from Titan, who whispers it against me, his breath hitting my neck and ear as he asks it. And it's not anger in his voice now. There's almost a laugh detectable in his soft whisper. I ignore the all-over body chill that runs through me. I can't let myself go there with Titan. Last time I did, I ended up married, with my stomach sore for weeks from being fucked so hard.

It was a really good feeling—but still.

"No harm for a woman to enjoy a good dicking, girl. You just got a hold of the wrong one," Leroy adds, spouting his wisdom again—which is starting to sound less and less wise.

"It's not just any... *dicking*... It's... Titan. He didn't want to go there with me, so I got him drunk and completely took advantage of him."

"Jesus," Leroy says.

"'Bout time you admitted it," Titan says, and maybe jail is a good place for him.

"If you like dick that much, darlin', I got some for you and trust me, it won't be whiskey-limp."

"Probably because you'll pump it full of Viagra."

"What in the fuck you saying?" Leroy asks, and then, proving he really is stupid, ignores the fact that Titan is twice his size and can grind him into dust. "I might be older, boy, but I'll mop the floor with you."

"I'm not your *boy*," Titan growls, trying to push around me. This is getting out of hand and escalating fast. It's worse because I see Sheriff Adams walking along the sidewalk. If he comes this way, suddenly the threat of jail for Titan seems all too real.

"You wouldn't work for me anyway, Leroy. I'm afraid only Titan will."

"No way," Leroy says, clearly disbelieving me. Titan, on the other hand, gets still and again some of his anger leaves. I can literally *feel* it. I have no idea how or why I can—I just know I do.

"Afraid so," I sigh sadly.

"You been missing my dick, wife?" Titan asks in my ear again. I have. I really have, but I'm not about to admit that, so I ignore him and concentrate on Leroy.

"You know what they say, Leroy."

"What's that?" he asks, eyeing me way too close—and since he's had his hand on my ass, that's saying something.

"Is there a problem here?" the sheriff asks, proving my luck is shit.

"Maybe, Adams," Leroy says. "Faith here has a husband, only I don't think she wants him. I think she's afraid of him."

"Is that true, Faith?"

Titan is being unusually quiet behind me. *Figures.* I have to make a split-second decision on if I want Titan to go to jail or not.

Damn it.

10

TITAN

I take a wait-and-see approach here. I have to admit I like having Faith close to me and I'm enjoying teasing her and the way she keeps trying to wade in the middle of me and this racist fuck, Leroy. I hate people like this asshole, throwing words out like he doesn't realize what he's saying, but the truth is there for anyone to read—or hear. I should punch him in the mouth and put an end to this shit, but for some reason I don't. I think that reason has everything to do with the way Faith keeps backing into me, inching closer every time Leroy shoots off at the mouth. Every time I whisper to her, her body shudders and it has a direct effect on my cock. Her ass keeps getting closer to my cock too, and that's an even better effect.

I put my hand on Faith's hip and grin when she jumps underneath my touch.

"Easy there," I whisper for her ears only and just like clockwork, that shudder runs through her a mere second later. I find myself smiling even with Leroy still breathing the same air as me.

"There's no problem, Sheriff Adams," Faith says and again she backs into me, her ass grazing against my slacks. My cock instantly pushes up as if reaching for her.

Jesus.

"Faith was just explaining how she married this ... *man* ... out of her love for—"

"Trouser snake," she sighs and she sounds so disgusted with herself that I can ignore Leroy's tone when he refers to me as a man.

"You two are married?" the sheriff asks, sounding surprised. He has every reason to be. I doubt Faith broadcast she was married and any man who is a man wouldn't have allowed her to work like she has been. Hell, we're not even married the way a man and a woman should be and I don't like that she has these ass-fucks looking at her like this.

I let *Leroy* explain to the sheriff how Faith and I are married and my claim she got me drunk. I can even smirk a little when he starts talking about my woman's—*Faith's*—love of 'trouser snakes'. One thing about it, being around Faith is never boring. It might be too much excitement for one man.

"I was just explaining to Faith that I'd be willing to help her out if she didn't want to stay married. I got more than enough to keep her happy."

"You're a horny old fool, Leroy. Faith, maybe we should go inside and talk," the sheriff says and I might have some respect for him. It's clear he has Leroy pegged.

"That won't be necessary," I tell the sheriff, getting tired of all of this. "My wife and I need to leave. We have things to discuss."

"I can't leave, Big Daddy. I have to work."

"Does he make you call him Big Daddy?" Leroy asks and, hand to God, I think the old geezer is getting a stiff one. Maybe the fucker doesn't need Viagra after all.

"It's a pet name," Faith grumbles.

"She gave it to me after she looked at my dick," I add helpfully. Her body stiffens for a moment and then she turns to look at me, shooting me an annoyed expression that makes me grin.

"That's what did it for you, wasn't it, sweet cheeks? You liked the size of *Daddy's* dick."

"That's it exactly," Faith says, her voice tight and there might be a smile on her face, but she's not happy—which, oddly enough, makes me happy.

"That's my girl. She does love my dick," I brag, pulling her into me.

"That I do," she mumbles, not sounding very pleased about it.

"I told you, if that's all it is, I got one for you, Faith. And I'll make it so you never want to run from me."

"I didn't say I ran," she defends.

"He showed up here and no one knew you were married. That seems to mean you ran," Leroy says, proving—I guess—that not all his brains are made of shit.

"I didn't run. I just decided I didn't want to be married. That's why I need the lawyer to get the divorce."

"Well, a woman shouldn't have to get married over her love of having a good—"

"Please don't say dicking anymore, Leroy," Faith says, interrupting him, and I laugh. Not a lot, but enough that Faith looks up at me with her eyes shooting daggers.

"How about I help you pay the lawyer and you can come stay with me? I'll show you how a real man takes care of his woman."

Okay, that's about all of this shit I'm going to take. Doesn't matter how fucking cute Faith is—and damn if she isn't. I'm actually enjoying most of this damn situation. I just need to punch Leroy so he stops talking and breathing. And I'm not real particular in which order that occurs—as long as it does.

"That's kind of you, Leroy, but I told you. It's only Big Daddy's that does it for me."

"You know that's right," I whisper to her again, but I might say it a little louder—just so the others can hear me. She turns to look at me fully, and there's a warning in her eyes. But I find I can't stop myself. "You couldn't get enough of it," I remind her, because the memories I've had of her prove that to be right. Fucking trouble is, I felt the same damn way about her pussy. "So, sorry, Leroy. You've lost out. It's only my dick Faith craves."

I smirk and I'm man enough to admit I'm getting great pleasure delivering that fact out there for all these assholes.

11

FAITH

"One dick is just as good as the other," Leroy says obstinately. Dear Lord, this keeps up there's going to be measuring tapes and egos involved. Of all of the ways I imagined meeting Titan again, spending an hour talking about his dick to other men wasn't it—at all. And for his part, Titan is enjoying this way too much. Which I'm finding annoying and I think it's about time to put an end to that.

"It's true, Leroy. You know what they say. Once you go black, you never go back."

The crowd is silent for a bit with that and I feel kind of proud of myself. I chance a look at Titan and I see shock there but he's so close to laughing. His eyes—deep pools of molten whiskey—are sparkling with it. Damn. *Why does he have to be so sexy?*

"Well." The sheriff clears his throat but doesn't say anything else. I'm pretty sure I've left him speechless.

"Darlin', you know what they say about white men," Leroy says. Man, he's just a dog with a bone—so to speak. He's refusing to give up. He should get an A for effort at the very least.

"What's that?" I ask, almost afraid to hear it.

"Once you come back to white, you've never had a fit so tight."

Well, shit. Score one for Leroy because I think he's stumped me.

"Jesus," Titan laughs.

"I don't think that's a thing, Leroy," I tell him as delicately as I can.

"It is," he replies, remaining stubborn.

Like a dog with a bone.

"If you're so happy with his—uh... with everything," the sheriff begins, "then why do you want a divorce?"

"Good question," Leroy adds.

"Can't wait to hear the answer to this one," Titan agrees and the smugness in his tone makes me go further than I'd planned.

"I need a divorce..." I grumble stubbornly, while I come up with my reply in my head.

"On what grounds?" the sheriff asks.

"Grounds?" I echo... *Hmm...*

"Yeah. On what grounds do you need a divorce? If he's threatening you I can step in," the sheriff says—perhaps a bit *too* eagerly.

"I'm not threatening her, you—"

"Fraud!" I nearly shout before Titan can call the sheriff a name that will end him up behind bars.

"Fraud?" There's a chorus of voices saying this to me, but Titan's is the one that sticks out the most. I should probably think twice about attempting the path that I'm about to walk down. I've never been the type to do that, however—which explains *so much* about my life.

"Fraud. Titan lied to me," I tell the sheriff and Leroy, and doing my best to ignore Titan completely.

"Lying is not really fraud, Faith," the sheriff says, rubbing the back of his neck.

"It is when they're lying to you about who they are."

"Darlin', maybe you aren't understanding about lying. You can lie, but it doesn't mean fraud really. Just means you got hold of a snake in disguise."

"It's fraud when he's pretending to be a man."

"What in the fuck are you saying now?" Titan growls.

For their part, the sheriff and Leroy are looking at Titan in disbelief. That's understandable. You can look at Titan and see he's all man. This is going to be a hard sell. But seeing the look of incredulity on Titan's face spurs me on.

"It's okay, Big Daddy. Leroy and Sheriff Adams are my friends. I feel comfortable telling them your secret."

"His secret..." the sheriff repeats, still staring at Titan like he can't believe it.

"Titan's really a woman," I deadpan and I'm pretty sure you can hear crickets around me.

"I'm going to wear your ass out," Titan groans and I ignore the full body shudder *that* gives me too.

"He's a chick?" Leroy says and he steps closer to Titan, looking at him closely.

"For fuck's sake. I am not," Titan growls.

The sheriff is smiling. I'm losing him. I pat Titan on the arm, but quickly take my hand back. Mostly because Titan looks and sounds like a giant grizzly bear right now and I'm afraid to leave my hand around him. In fact, I take a few steps away from him.

Better to be safe than sorry.

12

TITAN

"Faith, you're on dangerous ground here," I warn her and that's the only warning I give her.

I don't give two wasted fucks what these assholes think, but trying to strip me of my manhood—that's another thing. Maybe she needs a refresher course on just how real my dick is.

"He's a chick?" Leroy says again and the fucker gets too close and actually puts his hand on my chest. I push him away, deciding that I have indeed had enough of this bullshit.

"Back the fuck off, man," I growl.

"Touchy thing, aren't you?" Leroy laughs.

"Maybe he's PMSing," the sheriff jokes.

That's it.

"You liked it when I fed you my cock where people could watch us. Maybe I need to remind you just how much of a man I am," I tell her, going for the belt to my slacks. I see her swallow and her eyes dilate. She takes another step back from me, and that's probably the wisest thing she's done in her life.

"I actually want to see his... her... dick," Leroy says and the sheriff nods in agreement.

This makes me stop unzipping my pants. The last thing I want is Tweedle Dee and Tweedle Dum staring at my cock and trying to touch the damn thing. Just the thought of it makes him want to crawl up into my balls and hide.

"They made it out of his boobs," Faith says serenely, her face looking like she's discussing the Pope. Fuck, she's as crazy as her aunt who kept dancing with me at Aden's funeral... *Wedding...* Whatever.

"Out of his boobs?" Leroy clearly can't believe it. Maybe he has a few brain cells left.

"Holy shit," the sheriff adds.

"Oh yeah. He had huge boobs. What was it you said they were, Big Daddy? Triple Ds? He showed me a picture of them when he was confessing his secret to me. He easily rivaled Dolly Parton," Faith says and at this point, I'm just watching her mouth move to see what comes out of it next. Aden warned me to watch out for the Lucas clan—clearly I had no idea. It makes me wonder how in the hell White seems so freaking normal.

"Dolly has some great tits, that's for sure," Leroy responds and I wouldn't be surprised if he doesn't start foaming at the mouth. "You could bury your dick in those for days," he jokes.

"Yeah. That's enough," I growl. I bend down and wrap my arm around Faith's legs and throw her over my shoulder.

"Titan! Put me down!" she cries.

"See you later, boys," I mutter, praying I never do. "Time for me to take my wife home and show her just what a real man she did marry."

"You can't do this!"

"Sheriff! Help me!"

They either don't answer or her screaming drowns them out. I don't really care which one it is. I walk to my car, open the door and all but throw her inside.

"I'm not going anywhere with you," she huffs.

"You get out of this car you're in trouble. Because when I catch you, Faith—and I will—you'll be sorry. Now I've stood there for fucking-ever and let you convince two ass-fuck clowns that I'm not a man. I got to tell you, *wife,* I was mad before, but I'm at my limit now. So sit there like a good little girl or you won't like how I retaliate."

With that, I slam the door. I walk around to the driver's side and get the car started, pulling out as quickly as possible. The quicker I leave Buck-Stop in my rearview mirror, the better.

We get about a mile down the road when my car starts sputtering before coming to a complete stop.

"Uh... what's wrong?" she says, looking over at me cautiously.

"We're out of fucking gas," I growl, suddenly remembering why I was at that damn gas station in the first place.

"Whoopsie?" Faith says with a tentative grin and I really, *really* want to throttle her in that moment.

13

FAITH

I'm trying not to giggle as Joe pours gas into Titan's Caddy from a jug. We're standing beside the road. I called Joe's using Titan's cell-phone and here we are.

"That's two hundred dollars," Joe growls once his plastic jug empties.

"Two hundred fucking dollars? Are you kidding me? That wasn't even five gallons of gas."

"Most of the bill was for a tow. Actually that will be five hundred dollars."

"What the fuck?"

"You made me close my shop. You took my best worker away. You're lucky that's all I'm charging you," Joe says and I snort a little. I can't stop myself.

"Jesus. You take Visa?"

"Not out on the road I don't. Cash or check only."

"I don't have five hundred cash."

"Then we have a problem," Joe says, crossing his arms at his chest.

"We're about to," Titan says, his jawline going almost square. I read that as danger... lots of danger. I figure that means it's time for me to wade in again.

"Hey, Joe. Did you bring my stuff?"

"Yeah," he says, walking around to his old truck. He puts the gas can in the back and hands me the backpack I've been using to pack my clothes and crap in every day. I grab it and pull out my clothes first, 'cause damn do I want those. Then I rifle through the rest of it to find where I hid today's tips.

"Thanks, Joe," I tell him, right as I find my cash.

"I'm laying this out for you, Faith. You want to leave this guy, you can hop into my truck and I'll make sure the sheriff fixes it so he doesn't bother you again."

"He can try," Titan says and I wouldn't be surprised if he didn't start cracking his knuckles. Actually there's so much testosterone floating between these two a woman could get sick on it.

"I—"

"Faith," Titan says warningly. That's it, just my name, but it does get the message across. It doesn't matter. I was just staying in Buck-Stop to get some money together. If Titan wants to have a conjugal visit before I split again, I'm not against it.

Just the thought of that makes my female parts want to weep in happiness.

"I'm okay, Joe. Titan and I have a few things to work out," I tell him. Then I hand him the cash that was in my backpack—well, some of it. "Here, this is for Titan's bill. I'll get my money back from him, won't I, Big Daddy?"

He grunts in answer. Doesn't matter. I'll take his card if he wants to try and play that game. My Aunt Ida Sue always said there was more than one way to skin a cat, and I have to agree. I never understood why you would want to skin a cat, but whatever.

"Take care of yourself, Faith. You always got a job here if you want it," he says and that's sweet. I don't exactly want to be shaking my ass in a bikini in the cool Colorado air, but still it's sweet. I lean up on my tiptoes and deposit a kiss on Joe's weathered jaw. Before I'm firmly back on the balls of my feet, Titan is there with his arm around me. Joe takes him in and seems to be appraising him.

"See you later," Titan says, making his meaning clear. He wants Joe gone. His arm is so tight around my stomach it's a wonder I can breathe.

"You really a chick?" Joe asks and I can't stop the giggle.

"Fuck, no," Titan growls—which makes me giggle more.

"Didn't figure. Take care of her," Joe warns and dang it. I could get misty. I didn't think Joe liked me much. He's been nicer the last week, but still, he didn't talk much.

Titan doesn't bother replying. He's too busy pushing me back into his car.

"Bye, Joe!" I yell out the window, waving. Joe nods his head ever so slightly, but that's it. Then he hops in his truck and heads out.

I sit there watching his truck disappear and I got to admit, I'm a little sad about it. I was just getting comfortable in Buck-Stop. Whenever I take to the road again, I decide right then that I'm not stopping until I find another small town. It's much more peaceful than the bright lights of Vegas.

"Where do you live in this piece of shit town?" Titan asks and I frown.

"You don't like Buck-Stop?"

"Not a damn thing about it," he confirms and that makes me sad.

"Why?"

"Besides the obvious? There's nothing here." He shrugs. It's then I really look at Titan. He's wearing dress slacks, dark gray and perfectly creased. He's got a soft, deep purple button-up shirt on and the first few buttons are undone, letting you see his beautiful dark chest. He has on a gold chain. I've never liked that before, but on Titan it looks really good. He's got on his wedding ring—which surprises me, but then I'm wearing mine too. He's also got on one other heavy gold ring. It has a football on the side of it. He's driving a Cadillac and he practically oozes money. Every man

I've ever met like Titan has been bad news. Even if Titan is not, the differences between us are glaring. He oozes money. I struggle to buy dinner most days. He oozes city life and here I am perfectly happy in Buck-Stop and kind of wishing I didn't have to leave it.

"We could never be truly married," I tell him and I can't help it if my words sound kind of sad. I am sad.

"We are married, wife. Now where are you staying?"

"Truck stop down the road, why?"

"You're staying at a truck stop?" he growls.

"There's rooms for rent behind it for the night. It's not as bad as you're making it out to be," I grumble self-consciously. The truth is it's probably worse, but I'm not about to admit that.

"Give me directions."

I frown, but decide to go ahead. If I don't he's stubborn enough to drive around until I do. I've got to start figuring out how I'm going to get away from Titan. I can't stay with him. We're just too wrong for one another and I know how that works out. I've been there, done that and most definitely bought the T-shirt.

That's never going to happen again.

I touch my face gently as the past wars with my future. I need to leave Titan far behind me.

The farther the better.

14

TITAN

"You're right, Faith. This place is not as bad as I was thinking," I mutter, rubbing the side of my face as I take it all in. The door to her tiny room is practically pressed wood. It's been wet and not treated, so pieces of it have fallen off. I'm surprised it's even hanging on the hinges. An eighty-year-old grandmother could kick down this damn door. The inside is worse. There's paneled walls that look like something from an old seventies movie. There's a television on a table that is probably that old too. It's got dials on it, no remote control for that damn thing—not that it matters if the rabbit-ear antenna on the back is anything to judge by. The whole damn place smells stale and like the carpets have been flooded. The carpet is shit-brown, and when I say that it wouldn't surprise me if it was colored with actual shit. The bed... *Fuck... it's a damn water bed.* There's a mirror on the damn ceiling. The door to the bathroom is missing and you can see the dingy yellow toilet and a shower... I think it's supposed to match, but it looks more brown.

"Thank you," she says and she grins as she says it.

"It's worse."

"It's—"

"It's a shit hole," I tell her plainly.

"It's not that bad," she argues.

"Yeah, babe. It is."

"Whatever. You will have to sleep on the floor, I'm not giving up the bed."

"I'm not staying here."

"Oh. Even better. Later then," she says way too cheerfully.

"I'm not leaving you here, Faith."

"I'm not leaving here, period, Titan."

"You are."

"I'm not."

"You're getting your ass in my car and we're going back to Vegas."

"I don't like Vegas. I was leaving before I met you and I've left it now. What's more, I'm not going back," she says. She puts her hands on her hips like she's daring me to argue. She's sassy as fuck and damn if I don't like it.

"Where are you going, then?"

"I'm thinking Arkansas."

"*Arkansas*?" I was right the first time; the woman is fucking insane.

"Yeah. Little Rock."

"Do you know someone in Little Rock?"

"No. I just saw the name on my Atlas and I liked it." She shrugs like that's perfectly reasonable.

"Fine. We'll go back to Vegas and get a divorce and *then* you can go to Little Rock."

"I'm not going back to Vegas."

"We need a divorce," I remind her, frowning because for some reason I don't like using that word.

"So I can give you my number and when you get the papers drawn up, you can call me and I'll tell you where to send them."

"And you will sign them?"

"Of course I would. It's not like I want to stay married to you. I hate to break it to you, Big Daddy, but you aren't the world's best catch."

"You should try looking in the mirror." She frowns at me and I get the strangest notion that I hurt her feelings—which is crazy. "I'll get my guy in Vegas to fax me the papers you need to sign and bring them by tomorrow," I decide. That sounds like the simplest plan and really I don't think it's healthy for me to be around Faith. I alternate between wanting to kill her or fuck her. "Give me your number and I'll get out of your hair for the night."

"Uh... about that," she says and she's got that look on her face again. It's the look I've come to know as a warning. A warning she's about to start spouting bullshit.

"Warning, wife. It's been a rough few weeks trying to track your ass down. I've been on the road nonstop getting to you, and I've spent the day with other men being told I don't have a real dick. I'm not in the mood for more bullshit."

Her eyes narrow, but then she sighs and shrugs her shoulders in a small, delicate movement that has me watching the way it makes the muscles in her shoulders and neck work. She really is perfection—if you could harness that mouth and only use it for your dick.

"I don't have a phone," she mumbles.

"You don't have a phone?" I ask, totally not believing her. "Everyone has a phone."

"I *don't*."

"I call bullshit."

"Do you get that you're being annoying right now?"

"I get that you're lying to me."

"I'm not lying. I *had* a phone, but I don't anymore."

"What happened to your phone?" I ask her, wondering if this is going to be another out there in the twilight type of conversation.

"I dropped it in the toilet."

"You... When did this happen?"

"A few days after I got here. I dropped it and I just never got around to getting it replaced. I only talk to my sisters or some of my other family. I've been keeping in touch with Hope through the phone at Joe's. There didn't seem to be a big need to get another one."

"Didn't seem to be a need," I repeat, not believing what the fuck she's saying to me.

"If you are going to mimic everything I say, it's going to be a long night."

"A single woman alone should always carry a damn phone."

"I'm not single. I'm married."

"Quit playing stupid," I growl, tired of games.

"Maybe I'm not playing. I mean, I did marry you."

"It's good you remember, since your ass ran off," I remind her—to which she rolls her eyes. "Get your shit together. We'll find a hotel tonight and I'll call my lawyer in the morning."

"I—"

"I'm not arguing with you, Faith."

"I told you that you can go. You can call Joe's—"

"I'm rethinking that. I don't trust you not to be gone by morning. Now get your shit."

"I don't like you. I think I just need to make that clear."

"Message received."

"*Crystal* clear."

"Already got that message, wife, and don't really care. Now get your shit."

She gives me a look I figure is supposed to freeze off my dick and then stomps into the bathroom. I stand there watching her ass as she moves. I don't sit, because I'm afraid I'd pick something up in this hell hole that *might* make my dick fall off and I do all of this vowing never to touch tequila again.

15

FAITH

"I can't see as how this is much better than my place," I lie.

Titan found a Hampton Inn and Suites one town away from Buck-Stop, and then got a suite. It's probably a big step down for him. For me, it's nicer than any place I've ever lived or stayed in—with the exception of our hotel room in Vegas. This place is lush, for sure. There's a king size bed in one room with a bathroom you could have put my last apartment inside of. There's a door that opens off the bathroom that connects to a room with a sleeper sofa. I guess that's where he expects me to sleep; he doesn't seem like the type to give up the bed. There's a kitchenette, a huge television and attached desk. It's gorgeous, but there's no way I would admit that to him.

He grunts at me while taking off the blazer he's wearing. I remember the feel of that blazer and the smell of it... *the smell of him*. I gave it back to him after we came back to my room at the truck stop and I threw my own clothes on. Suddenly I miss it. That thought brings a sigh to my lips, but I hold it in and try to ignore the way the shirt he's wearing stretches across his broad shoulders and chest with his movement. Titan might be a jerk, but he's hot—as in panty melting hot.

Too bad he's an asshole.

"I'm thirsty," I inform him.

"There's a sink with water," he says, not even bothering to look up at me.

Definite asshole.

"I'd like a real drink, from the vending machines," I grumble. I'd prefer an alcohol-type drink but there's no in-room bar and I don't think alcohol and Titan mix really well together.

I learned that lesson the hard way.

"The only way you get that is if I go with you and I'm too damn tired to leave this room. That makes your choices limited."

"So you're saying I'm a prisoner here?"

"Until I get a hold of my attorney tomorrow and he gets me the papers you need to sign so we can get our divorce, then yes."

"You're just being mean," I mumble, clearly pouting. He ignores my pout and he does this by securing the remote control and turning on the television.

"Mean is telling people a man's dick isn't a dick but fucking titty fat," he grumbles, stretching out on the bed. He kicks his shoes off and pulls two pillows behind him to lie on. He's got his hands behind his head, elbows bent, looking like he owns the world. He might have a point but I ignore it. Instead, I rifle through my bag and find my shorts and a cami that I usually sleep in. Then I bundle them up in my arms and look at my prison warden, daring him to argue.

"I'm taking the first shower." I expected him to respond, but he doesn't. He ignores me and I take that for a yes. I stomp off, leaving him to his television.

Getting in the shower, I notice yet another difference between the hotel that Titan picked and the one I was staying at. The hot water is actually hot and the water is crystal. I'd never admit it where Titan could hear me, but there were times I couldn't wash in the water at the truck stop. It would come out more brown than anything and I'd go into the garage early and clean up there. Which means I lose myself in the shower. I should feel guilty that

I take all of the hot water from Titan, but I can't seem to. No one made him follow me and they sure didn't make him hold me hostage in a hotel room—even if that hotel room is fantastic.

"You better be in here," Titan growls, barging in the door just as I grab a towel. I've never been extremely shy about my body and it's kind of stupid to worry about it around Titan, since we know each other—in the biblical sense. Still, for modesty's sake I do hold the towel in front of me, hiding my boobs and hoo-hah.

His large frame kind of stops mid-movement. His face registers surprise and his dark whiskey eyes center on me and put off enough heat that I'm almost afraid they can burn me. His gaze is trained on my body and I'm wondering if I should worry they could catch the towel I'm wrapping around me on fire. When it's clear he's not going to look up, I almost giggle.

"See something you like, Big Daddy?"

"Can you cut out the nickname shit?"

"You don't like being called Big Daddy?"

"Not especially," he says, letting his annoyance shine bright.

"I'll be sure to do it more often. Was there a reason you busted in here?"

"You've been in the shower for over an hour."

"Was I under a time limit?" He crosses his arms and stares at me, but says nothing. "I'm not good at mind reading. *Was* I supposed to adhere to some sort of unannounced schedule?"

"Do you always start talking prissy when you get pissed?"

"Believe it or not, I never got pissed much until you came into my life."

"I don't believe it." He grins.

"Suit yourself."

"What if I wanted to shower?" he asks, and it's clear he's not going to leave, so I walk around him to the sink and grab the toiletries bag I left there earlier.

"Then have at it... *Big Daddy.*"

"I doubt there will be any hot water left," he says and since it was cold when I turned it off, I'm pretty sure he's right.

"Oh well, we can't have everything, obviously. If we could I'd be in Arkansas."

"And I'd be single," he agrees and that kind of hurts, but I ignore it. Not like I wanted to be married to him. Still, no girl wants to feel like being married to her is one of the worst things that could happen to a man.

I decide to shut him out and since he won't leave, towel off. He's seen my body before and obviously if being married to me is so horrible, doesn't care to repeat any of the things we did together. I prop my leg up on the toilet and begin drying and it's then I feel my skin warm. I look up and Titan is staring at me and he's not bothering to hide the hunger on his face. It makes me feel flushed, confused and more than a little turned on.

"Titan?" I ask and I ignore how husky my voice sounds.

"On second thought, a cold shower sounds good," he growls.

Then it's my turn to watch as he sheds his clothes and jumps under the cool spray. I have to force myself not to watch the entire show. The look on his face and his obviously hard cock all spell trouble with a capital T. That's the only reason I throw on my clothes and all but run out of the room, unable to play it cool any more. I grab the comforter and a pillow off the bed and go to the sofa. I lay down on it without bothering to pull out the mattress it hides. I'm determined to be unavailable when Titan gets out of the shower. I know sleep will be a long time coming—for one thing, it's still early. I vow, however, that I'll pretend I'm asleep if Titan comes around.

I don't think I can talk to him right now. There's just no way, not while my mind is full of pictures of him naked.

16

TITAN

"What are you doing?" Faith grumbles. Her voice sounds sleepy, but I'd lay odds on the fact that she wasn't really asleep. I've pulled her up against my body, her legs hanging off one of my arms and her neck and head hanging off the other. Her ass is rubbing against my stomach and I wish it was a little lower—even if I shouldn't.

I have been remembering our wild night of sex—*our wedding night*—repeatedly while trying to find Faith. Each memory I began having was better and more explicit than the one before. Still, I was way too drunk to have terrific recall. Mostly I remembered the things we did and said. Details were indeed fuzzy. The glimpses I got of her body in the bathroom earlier—of that fucking fantastic ass and those cock-stand inducing legs—heated through my system with the force of a wildfire, burning me from the inside out. Faith is danger and I'd be wise to leave her alone... Instead I'm carrying her to my bed and giving new meaning to the term *playing with fire*.

"You're not sleeping on the couch," I tell her and if my voice sounds pissed it's her fault.

"You're giving up the bed?" she says, her voice filled with pleasure. "That's so sweet. I may have misjudged you, Titan. We should begin again. We can be friends this time," she whispers, her face burrowing into my neck as she loops her arms around me. I roll my eyes, not bothering to reply. I don't understand women, never really pretended to, but this one is in a category all her own and I *really* don't get her. I put her on the left side of the bed and then walk around to the other one and slide under the covers. "Titan!" she shrieks as I pull the covers up over us.

"Tone it down, woman. You'll have management after us." I yawn out the words. I've been out of the shower for hours. I've been watching television and waiting for my body to warm up after the cold water. Now I'm tired, still cold and so damned horny my dick aches. All of these things are Faith's fault, so I'm not fooling with her shit.

"You can't get in bed with me!" she argues and again she's *shrieking*. I open my eyes to look at her, all the while trying to ignore how good she looks with her hair rumpled from lying on the couch, her tank top molded to her body and giving me hints of cleavage and holding her tits like a fucking second skin.

"But I am. Now can you crank it down a few hundred notches and let's go to sleep."

"I... But you said you were giving me the bed and going to the couch."

"I didn't say that. You *assumed* that. And you know what they say about assuming."

"Then I'll go back to the sofa," she argues.

"And then you'll run away in the middle of the night. Been there, *wife*. Not doing it again."

"Oh come on. I told you I'll stay until you get the papers from your lawyer."

"I don't trust you."

"I don't like you."

"I could remind you of exactly what you did like about me," I tell her, my voice a dare I hope she takes me up on.

"In your dreams, Big Daddy," she mumbles. "I'll just go in—"

I reach out and grab her hand and pull her to me. She falls

against my chest, leaving our faces a mere inch away from one another.

"I already told you, I don't trust you. You'll stay in this bed so I know where you are."

"You can't be serious. Did you forget that I left our hotel room while you *were* next to me in Vegas?"

"I'm glad you brought that up. I thought of that," I tell her and I have a hard time keeping the smile off my face.

"You did?" she asks and the worry in her tone lets me know I didn't succeed in hiding my smile at all. *Oh well.* I keep my hand around her wrist, not letting her go and lean over to the nightstand to open the drawer. While Faith was showering earlier, I hid my little surprise there. I feel around in the drawer and when my fingers wrap around the cool metal I loop a finger in it and pull it out. I flop over to my back and grin at a Faith whose eyes have gone large and round in shock and maybe a little worry.

She should be worried.

I dangle a pair of handcuffs, letting them swing back and forth.

"I brought you a little gift since I know how much you like games in the bedroom."

"No. No way in hell, Titan. You will not—" Before she can finish the sentence I've closed the loop of the handcuff around her wrist—letting it replace my hand. "—I can't believe you did that," she cries.

"Believe it, sweet cheeks." I laugh, connecting the other cuff to my wrist. I hold back another laugh when she beats her hand against my chest. It's not easy though. For some reason, right now I'm happier than I've been... since the night I got married.

Shit.

17

FAITH

I come awake slowly, feeling warm and heated all the way to my bones. The mattress beneath me is just as warm... *toasty even.* It must have some kind of heated mattress pad on it. I don't remember that from last night, but this morning I'm thankful. Plus, it's so soft. I'll say one thing about my soon to be ex-husband, he sure has great taste in hotel rooms. I stretch, knowing there's no way I'm going to go back to sleep—despite the warmth.

"Sweetheart, you keep wiggling like that and we're going to have a repeat performance of our wedding night."

I freeze, locking my body into place as all the memories of last night slam into my head. I ignore Titan's voice, the vibration, the deep timbre and gruffness of it that makes wetness ease between my thighs. He might be sexy, but he's an asshole.

I'm definitely awake now, however, and as awareness hits me, I realize that I'm lying on Titan, not the mattress. I know that because when I look down it's into the whiskey-colored depths of Titan's eyes and they're heated. It's his cock which is rock hard, pushing against my center—at exactly the *right* spot.

Houston... I think we have a problem.

"You don't have any clothes on," I whisper, still kind of drowning in his eyes and the way they sparkle.

"Nice of you to notice."

"Couldn't help but notice, since little Titan is poking me."

"Maybe you need reminded that there's nothing little about my cock," he says. I watch as his lips slide into an easy grin, those thick beautiful lips stretching little by little, and as the smile forms his eyes seem to sparkle even more. I feel nervous flutters in my stomach. The smile has that much of an effect.

"I don't think that would be wise," I tell him, but inside I hate myself for not saying yes. I want him. I want to relive what we did together. I've thought about it nonstop since I left Vegas. A part of me—a very big part—wants to throw caution to the wind and agree. Titan moves his hand to reach up and push some of my hair out of my face. The simple gesture is sweet in a way that makes that nervous flutter in my stomach deepen, but it also causes the handcuff to rattle against my wrist—reminding me of why I can't give in to my body's demands where Titan Marsh is concerned.

"It's okay. After all, we're married," he jokes but the moment has passed and I ignore the sparkle in his eye because I'm slowly coming back to reality.

"Not for very long since you're supposed to be calling your lawyer," I respond. Then I hold up my hand, bringing his up as I do it. I shake it slightly. "Can you undo these? I need to go pee."

He frowns, the light dimming in his eyes—which is sad, but necessary. He shifts underneath me—a movement that causes his cock to push deeper against me. It takes a supreme effort, but I ignore how good that feels. His hand shuffles through the drawer and comes out with a key. In a movement that is too practiced and smooth, he undoes the lock. It would be best not to dwell on that particular talent that Titan has.

"Your wish is my command," he says and I push up from him, sliding off his body.

"Thanks," I mumble and walk quickly to the restroom. It takes effort not to run. I need away from him that much. Once I shut the door, I collapse against it. My heart is hammering against my chest. I'm not ready for Titan. My sisters are right. I am stupid when it comes to men. You would think after the mess I was in with Brad I wouldn't have even looked at another man—let alone marry him. I go to the sink and look in the mirror. "You're a stupid girl," I tell my reflection as I splash water on my face.

Through the door I hear Titan moving around. That nervousness in my stomach tightens. I made a huge mistake with Brad. He was a pretty boy and did his best to impress me at every turn—until he didn't. I thought he was strong; someone I could trust. He was as weak as they come. He taught me a lesson and he taught it hard. I will never forget that lesson; it's deep inside of me now. It bubbles to the surface when I least expect it.

It surfaced the morning I left Titan and Vegas in my rearview mirror. That was the main reason I ran away without a word. Now, standing in front of a mirror and the harsh florescent light of the bathroom, I can feel that same fear bubbling up.

There's only one major difference.

I'm not thinking of running right now. I'm thinking of going back in there and climbing into Titan's bed and taking him up on his offer—and that brings a fear bigger than anything I've ever felt. I have to be out of my mind.

But am I?

Titan is nothing like Brad, as near as I can tell. Brad is a "pretty" boy, smooth as a California coastline. There's nothing smooth about Titan, except the way his body moves as it powers into me—which is better not to think about right now. Still, Titan is rough around the edges. He doesn't feed you lines; he just plain tells you like it is. I never wonder where I'm standing when it comes to Titan. With Brad I always did—even when I thought I came first to him.

I shut down my thoughts. I have to.

I'm actually considering....

What? Keeping Titan? He tracked me down to get a divorce. Even if I wanted to keep him, he doesn't want me.

That reminder is like a slap in the face and brings me back down to earth quick. I turn on the shower with a shake of my head. Titan will get in touch with his lawyer and have papers for me to sign and it will be over. Then I'll jump in my car and head to Arkansas.

I'll leave Titan behind and I'll do it for good this time.

I have to.

18

TITAN

I hear the shower come on and close my damn eyes. There was a moment there I thought Faith was going to take me up on my offer. It was an offer I had no business making, but one I hoped like hell she'd say yes to. Fuck, the time for thinking with my dick should be over—but here I am. I have no excuses, absolutely none. I'm not a young kid hitting the field with a buffet of pussy waiting for me to fill up my plate and come back for seconds. There's never been a shortage of women in my life. I've enjoyed many, but Faith is different. Sounds fucking crazy as hell, but it's true. I've never had this strong of a reaction to a woman before. Maybe it's because we've had sex and I can't remember all of it. Maybe it's because what I can remember is fucking phenomenal and I want more—only this time I want to do it sober and savor every second. That's not going to happen today. I rub my dick, wishing this morning had gone down differently. It's probably for the best. I have to get my head in the game. It's time to go about making my wife an *ex*-wife instead of trying to get between her legs again.

I reach over and grab my cellphone and sift through my contacts until I find my attorney's private number.

"Damn it, man, it's 5:30 in the morning. This better be good."

I smirk at the sound of annoyance in Marty's voice. Asshole has probably been awake for hours. Although, I'm going to be honest, I had no idea it was so early. I was more interested in making my dick happy.

"I found my wife," I tell him, not bothering to call him a liar or finding out how long he's been awake.

"I figured that was it, since I never hear from you unless you want something from me."

"You don't complain when you cash my retainer check every month, asshole," I remind him, putting him in his place. I don't let people talk down to me, and I sure as hell refuse to let someone on my payroll do that shit.

"I'm getting ready to raise that bill. What do you need from me?" he asks, finally getting down to business.

"Can you fax me whatever Faith needs to sign to make this annulment happen?"

"All shit aside, Titan, man, are you sure this is what you want?" he asks and, without realizing it, my gaze travels to the closed bathroom door.

"Why would you even ask that shit?" I ask Marty, but I know. Marty doesn't like the plan Cora and I have in play. Marty might try to act like a mercenary motherfucker, but he never quite pulls it off.

I'm starting to wonder if I can.

"Because at least you get along with this bitch, which is more than I can say for the future Mrs. Marsh. Maybe this happened for a reason," he answers, being plain spoken—like he always is with me.

"It did and that reason was a starved dick, a hungry pussy and a fuckload of tequila." I lay it out for him, but I feel a little guilty talking about Faith like that.

Which is crazy. I didn't say anything that wasn't true... mostly.

"I'll fax the annulment papers. Have Faith sign them and I'll get them filed. You can be a free man by the end of the week."

"Sounds good. Thanks, Marty."

"I wouldn't thank me. Basically I'm just doing this so you can get married again and really fuck up your life. I'm doing you no favors," he adds and I rub the back of my neck in frustration.

"Nice, man—real nice."

"Just calling it like I see it. Give me the damn number."

I get out of bed and go to the desk. It takes me a minute to find the binder with the hotel information, but I get it and then give him the number. We exchange a few more words and I hang up.

Walking back into the main room, I can't stop myself from staring at the bathroom door. I try to get Marty's words out of my head. This is all for the best. Faith and I had one night of drunken sex after a very big mistake.

That's it.

19

FAITH

"What are you doing?" Titan asks for the hundredth time.

We are at a Waffle House, and after breakfast I pulled out the papers Titan gave me and started going over them. That was about fifteen minutes ago and Titan keeps asking me what I'm doing—which means I haven't read very much at all and he's starting to annoy me.

"I'm trying to read—if you would quit interrupting me," I grumble.

"What is there to read? You just sign the damn thing and this is done," he growls. I frown up at him.

Maybe it's silly, but his constant griping about these papers and wanting our marriage to end is really starting to hurt my feelings. I mean, come on, I have my faults, but geez Louise. I'm not *that* bad.

"I'm reading because it's a legal document. My parents didn't teach me a lot—mostly because my mom was crap and tied my dad in knots. My dad was always trying to undo those knots and did that until the day he died, so there wasn't much room for him to teach us life's lessons. Which means, *Big Daddy*, those lessons came harsh at the hands of fate—who is a fickle bitch at best. Still, one of those life lessons was you don't sign any kind of contract unless you read it first. So, and I'm only repeating myself here because you've been an ass, I'm reading."

"What's to read?"

"I'm ignoring you, but the more you talk the longer it will take me to read," I warn him. I hear him groan under his breath and want to giggle. I can admit it—at least to myself—it's fun to annoy Titan. When I finish reading, I get this feeling of dread. It sits in the pit of my stomach. I pick up the pen and stare at the line where my signature is supposed to go.

I'm feeling a million things and it's probably not fair to Titan, but the biggest one of those is feeling like a failure. I can hear Hope and Charity condemning me now, telling me how my life has just been one major screw-up after another. I can even see the looks on their faces. I gaze up at Titan. He's a good man. I'm convinced of that. I've spent my time with bad and Titan is completely different. If I were ever going to get married, I'd want it to be to a man like him—*a good man*.

"I'm dying of old age here, Faith."

A good man is an asshole.

"This says I agree the marriage was a mistake," I tell him, frowning and trying to read his face. As a blackjack dealer, I got really good at reading people's emotions and find their "tells." Titan is pretty closed off, but right now I see disbelief on his face and more than a little bit of anger.

"Fuck yeah. You going to tell me it wasn't?"

"Well, I mean, I don't know. It could be, because Lord knows you're not exactly sweet and tender."

"You have got to be fucking me."

I bite my lip at his choice of words and the images they evoke.

"Who's to say though? Maybe the marriage wasn't a mistake. We might make a great married couple."

"You really are fucking with me right now," he growls and I cross my hands at my chest.

"Why is it so hard to believe that being married to me wouldn't be the end of the world?" I huff defensively.

"Because I'm engaged!" he growls and my body goes completely still. It feels like lead, solid and hard to move.

"You had sex with me when you were engaged?" I whisper, almost choking on the words. I thought Titan was a good man. I felt inside of me that he was. I liked him!

I am a fool.

My sisters are right; I just keep making mistake after mistake.

"I was drunk! I didn't know what I was doing. Hell, you could have been a hooker off the street," he growls.

And the blows just keep coming. Trouble is, this one cuts deep. I feel it slice through me like a hot knife. I swallow down the hurt and the damaged pride. I don't have time to feel those, and I'd never let anyone see it anyway—especially Titan.

"Who's your fiancée? Does she know about me?"

"I—"

"You know what, never mind. It's none of my business."

"Will you just sign—"

"You know what? It *is* my business. I bet she doesn't know anything about me. I bet she's just laughing and happily planning a wedding to a man who is a lying, cheating, cretin!"

"Cretin?"

"That's what I said, buckaroo. And if the stupid fits wear it! I can't believe you. You made me a scarlet woman and I didn't even know! Your fiancée will hate me!"

"She won't. But does it even matter? Not like you will ever meet her."

"So *that's* your game? What Mrs. Big Daddy don't know won't hurt her?"

"Will you stop getting upset over nothing?" he sighs. "You're starting to attract attention."

"I don't care! You just told me you were engaged to get married to another woman and married me instead. How do you think that makes me feel, Titan?"

"Ask me if I care, Faith," he dares me rather bitchily and

further proving that, despite my first assessment, Titan is *not* a good guy. He's a complete and utter asshole.

"Ask me if I'm going to give you an annulment, Titan?"

"What are you saying?"

"I'm saying, *husband,* that I'm going to protest the annulment. I'm not giving it to you."

"Why in the hell not?"

"I'm doing this for your fiancée!" I proclaim, standing up.

"What the fuck are you talking about?" he barks and there are several gasps of shock around us. Good! I hope they throw him out for using coarse language. It'll serve him right!

"I'm saying that if you're married to me, you can't break another woman's heart. One who probably cares for you. So I'm not giving you an annulment!"

"You can't keep me married to you, Faith. I can get a divorce on my own."

"Then go ahead and file for a divorce! Have the papers sent to my Aunt Ida Sue in Texas. Hope can give you the address," I yell, heading for the exit.

"Where in the fuck are you going?" he asks.

"I'm going back to my jeep in Buck-Stop and then I'm driving to Arkansas!"

"You don't have a way there and I'm sure as hell not taking you," he returns, his voice as loud and as angry as mine—but his sounds scarier.

"I didn't ask you to, Big Daddy. I'm fine on my own!"

"I can drive you, sweetheart," a giant bear of a man says from the corner. One look at him and I peg him as a trucker. He has a faded blue Ford baseball cap on, a flannel long-sleeved shirt with the sleeves rolled up, faded jeans and a white T-shirt—with what I hope are coffee stains. He's got a long brown beard, and a mop of hair just as long.

"You will not," Titan orders him.

The man stands up and he might not be quite to Titan's height, but he's big and he's wide. He's not all muscle like Titan, and that beer belly he's sporting has not one sign of Titan's perfect abs, I'm sure, but he's not going to back down and he's got one ace in the hole. There's a state policeman at the booth beside him and he comes out, giving Titan a look that can't be misinterpreted.

"You got this, David?" the trucker says and it is clear David is the state police when he comes to stand in front of Titan.

"I got it. In fact, I think I'll give the little lady a ride myself," the cop says and I smile—aiming that smile of victory directly at Titan.

"Faith, you leave like this and you'll regret you ever met me."

"Too late, Big Daddy. I already do!" I tell him and then I look at the state policeman. "Um... I need my stuff out of *his* car." I smile, pointing at a very pissed-off Titan. Not that I care.

Titan Marsh is *not* my problem anymore. He can go hang out with all the other scummy, skeezy, lying cheaters.

And when his fiancée finds out about me, I hope she kicks him in the balls.

20

TITAN

I keep replaying shit in my head. I have for two days. I *still* don't know exactly what happened. Now, this is nothing new when it comes to Faith, but never have I been more confused than I am right now. It seemed so simple. She signs the annulment papers, I turn them in and we both get on with our lives. I forgot one thing.

Nothing is ever simple when it comes to Faith.

I couldn't go after her immediately, not since she conveniently had state police protection. It has taken me two days to catch up with her. I'm following her Jeep now down a back road somewhere close to the Oklahoma border. There's no rhyme or reason to the roads that Faith keeps taking. Hell, I swear sometimes she manages to make a complete circle. She literally comes to a stop sign and turns right, goes to another one and turns left and ends up back at the original one. It's the craziest thing I've ever seen. At first, I thought it was because she caught me tailing her. The more it happened, the more I'm sure this has something to do with Faith's own brand of crazy.

It's almost dark before she stops for the night. I've been following her for at least fourteen hours, watching her from a distance and getting gas when she goes inside to eat or at a station.

It hasn't been easy, but I've done damn good at it. I'm starting to think I should have been a P.I. instead of a football player. Luckily, her Jeep gets horrible gas mileage compared to my Caddy. She pulls into a small motel that is literally called Highway 69 Motel. The road we are on is not Highway 69, not even close. That should be a warning sign to the woman that she should keep driving. But it doesn't surprise me that she goes in to register. I pull into the parking lot only after she goes inside. Then I park my car and get out. Every bone and joint I have pops as I finally stand. Too many years of football have made trips like this painful. I lean against her hood and wait.

It doesn't take long before she comes outside singing—*singing*—and doesn't look up. When she gets just a foot away from me I figure if I don't speak up she's going to run straight into me. How this girl survives on her own, I have no idea.

"Hello, *wife*."

She lets out a startled scream, jumps in place slightly and then stares at me. She's got sunglasses on that hide her eyes from me. I frown, wishing they were gone. There's no reason for her to have them. It's nearly dark outside.

"Look what the cat drug in," she mumbles. "I was wondering when you would show up."

"You knew I would?" I can't help but ask.

"Bad pennies usually do. How's your fiancée?" she says, her voice full of sarcasm.

"Don't know. Haven't talked to her."

"Haven't... Is that normal?"

"Pretty much."

"That's sad. She deserves better, but then maybe she should count her lucky stars. If she knew what a dick you were it might hurt her."

"I doubt it, since we are just friends."

"Just friends?"

"Pretty much. Not that I owe you a reason, but Jacey and I are marrying for business reasons only. Don't know a hundred percent, and don't care enough to ask, but I'm pretty sure Jacey would rather be marrying you and what you're packing between your legs than what I have."

She stands there and it takes her several minutes to come up with the correct answer. When it does her whole stance changes.

"You're getting married for business reasons?"

"People have gotten married for less." I shrug, the entire subject making me uncomfortable.

"That's so... cold..." she whispers and her voice sounds like she's in mourning.

"What do you care? You said you didn't like marriage, remember?" I remind her of the night we met.

"I don't. Still... Whatever. Listen, I'm not signing your papers. I've thought about it and I can't."

"Why the fuck not?"

"Because I can't sign my name and swear what it wants me to," she mumbles.

"Like what?"

"Well for one, we didn't lie, so fraud is out."

"Okay, then what else?"

"It mentioned force. Neither one of us can claim that," she says logically and I try to keep from yelling at her, but it's getting harder.

"And?"

"Incest. I think that one is out clearly. I mean you can look at us and tell that."

"Jesus." Her mind fucking scares me.

"And it said we qualify for an annulment if we're previously married and didn't get a legal divorce before. Titan, I'm not married—though I can't say for sure if you are or not. I mean, you have a fiancée that I didn't know about. Who's to say you don't go around collecting wives like other people collect stamps?"

"No one collects postage stamps anymore, Faith."

"My Aunt Ida Sue does," she defends.

"Your aunt is bonkers," I say with a shrug.

"That's not nice, Big Daddy. *She* likes you."

"Yeah? I know my ass has still got the bruises from the way she kept pinching it."

"Well, in her defense, you do have a nice ass." Faith smiles and pulls her sunglasses off her face, holding them loosely in her hand. Even in the pale evening light and muted glow of the parking lot I can see her eyes sparkle. She's beautiful... *Damn it.*

"Okay, so no on any of those reasons, but woman, you can't deny we were both drunk off our asses and shouldn't have made a big decision like getting married."

"Maybe... But I can't say I didn't realize what we were doing." She shrugs.

"Are you saying you wanted to get married?"

"No! Well... I don't think so. It seemed like a good idea at the time," she ends. And all of a sudden, I feel like I've been sucker punched.

"And I always thought an annulment was if you haven't had sex, but when I read it said if we had kids, it would recognize them as being legitimate even if we get an annulment and..."

I feel like I can't breathe.

"Are you fucking pregnant?" I bark and she jumps.

"No. I don't think so... but I can't be sure yet."

"So we take you to the doctor. I don't see how you can be pregnant. We used protection."

"Except for that one time in the shower," she reminds me and until that moment I hadn't remembered the shower. At her words flashes come in my mind. Images of us standing in the shower, her back to my front. My hands full of her tits while my cock is pushing inside of her, me biting into her neck as her body pushes against me and I thrust deep...

Fuck.

"We'll go get a test and find out."

"I'm tired, Titan."

"Tonight we'll rest. We can do the test tomorrow."

Her eyes narrow at me and I see the distrust there.

"You're planning on staying in my room with me, aren't you?"

"Yeah."

"You get those handcuffs near me, Titan, and I'm going to shove my foot so deep in your ass you will never walk right again," she threatens.

For some reason, my lips spread into a half smile and I want to laugh.

"Point made, wife. Point made."

21

FAITH

I look at a sleeping Titan and wonder for the millionth time what in the world I'm doing. I should just sign the annulment papers and move on. I don't know why I can't bring myself to do it. Every time I grab the pen to sign them, my sister Hope is in my head telling me what a failure I am. Charity is right there with her. Overshadowing them is thc voice of my mother and the fear that I'm just like her.

The strangest thing about it is by trying not to be her—I'm becoming her.

I had my period just last week. Why would I even bring up the possibility that I could be pregnant? I'm on birth control; I'm not pregnant. Sure, it was stupid to have unprotected sex, but I got drunk in Vegas and married a stranger. I think we can agree I wasn't smart that whole weekend, but it's time I start at least trying to be smarter.

It's time I put everything behind me. I left Vegas to start over and starting over means leaving Titan behind me too.

I don't stop to consider what I'm doing. I've been thinking too much tonight as it is. I reach up to touch the side of Titan's face. He really is beautiful. He's rough around the edges, but sleek and sexy... *powerful*. He's got lines on his face that deepen when he laughs or smiles and his eyes haunt me, even when he's not near. I love the almost amber color in their brown depths. I love the way they make me feel heated, make me feel... *alive*.

He mumbles in his sleep, but he doesn't move. That's okay, I don't specifically want him to wake up right now. If he wakes up, I might chicken out or at the very least he'll take control. I like when Titan takes control, but I want to play too.

I move so I'm between his legs, stretched over his body. Then I place gentle kisses down Titan's chest. The salty masculine taste of him bursts in my mouth as I touch the tip of my tongue against his skin. Titan moans and I stop to see if he'll wake up. His body moves and shifts under me. I can feel his cock pushing upwards, moving—showing me at least part of him is awake. His hand comes up and rests in my hair and I lift my gaze to his face, thinking I'm already caught—but he's clearly asleep. I close my eyes and lay my head against his stomach for a minute. I love the way his hand feels holding me like this. As weird as it seems, that's what I remember most about our night together, the way his fingers would curl into my hair and hold on while he came. It had the power to make me feel sexy, erotic and beautiful all in one.

When it's clear that he's not going to wake up, I carefully move so I'm sitting back on my knees between his legs. My eyes go to his cock and I couldn't look away if I wanted to. Titan is so beautiful he could rival any male model out there. His body is that exquisite, but it's big, strong, almost raw, and athletic in a way I've never seen in a man before. And his cock... I've said before how big, wide, and heart-stoppingly demanding it can be. There's no way I can take him completely in my mouth, but that's not going to stop me from trying.

If I'm going to say goodbye to Titan, I'm going to do it in a way he will never forget.

22

TITAN

I've been dreaming of Faith nonstop since that night in Vegas. So it's no surprise that it takes me a minute to figure out that I'm not dreaming. That it is Faith's tongue licking against my shaft, Faith's breath heating up my already overheated balls, and Faith's mouth my cock finally slides inside of.

As she closes her lips and sucks me hard, I can't stop a groan. *First-fucking-class.* I've never experienced anything like it. I thought the memories were embellishing things, making the memories better than the real thing. With Faith humming around my dick, I know I was wrong.

My fingers slide through the blond strands of her hair, tightening and curling against her head as she holds me tight and slides her lips down my cock. I force myself to keep my eyes open so I can watch her. Watch as inch by inch my cock disappears into her hot, wet mouth, filling her until she can't take it anymore and my head pushes deep in her throat. She takes it until she comes close to gagging around it and then backs off. Faith does this several times and then she shifts her gaze so she looks up at me.

Fuck me.

I was wrong, it could get better. Her eyes holding mine while she sucks me is infinitely better. There are things I want to say, but every time I start to open my mouth ... I am a loss of what to say. This is Faith. A woman who has gotten under my skin, but also a woman I'm here to get to sign annulment papers. All I really know right now is that I don't want her to stop. So that's what I give her, even if it's lame.

"Don't stop, Faith. Don't fucking stop," I moan, my head going back in pleasure as she palms my balls, squeezing them gently. She moves back up my shaft and again I force my head up to look at her. She lets my cock go with a loud "pop" that echoes in the room.

"You like that, Big Daddy?" she grins, looking way too pleased with herself.

That nickname she's given me, Christ she's a nut. It makes me smile, at times it makes me laugh and sometimes it makes me want to shake her. Still, I find I like it, even if I have no idea why.

"Can't you tell?" I challenge her, thrusting my cock up slightly to emphasize my answer.

"Oh, I could tell," she smiles, kissing the head and then pushing her tongue through the pre-cum that has gathered.

"You got too many clothes on, woman," I mumble, my brain slowly going to mush as she continues to play with me—her tongue teasing me, her soft little hand stroking me.

I find her shirt and begin pulling it up her body. She moves away from me and lets go of my cock long enough to help me strip her. I throw the shirt down on the floor and instantly wrap my hands around her breasts—squeezing them. I feel her body tremor in reaction and that makes my cock throb almost as much as her mouth did.

She likes my touch.

I squeeze the full mounds, and I don't do it gently. There has to be a sting of pain in my grip. Faith doesn't seem to care. In fact, her head goes back, those long blond tresses falling down around her like a veil, so long they tease against my legs. She takes a shuddering breath as her eyes close and my hands move from her breasts, across her ribs and finally to her hips, clenching and biting into them as I watch her tongue dart out to lick her lips.

So fucking sexy.

"Naked. I want you naked, Faith."

"But—"

"Now," I order, leaving no room for argument. She stares at me for a minute and then shifts so she can take off her shorts and underwear.

I thought the view couldn't get better. I discover I'm wrong. I sit up, resting against the back of the headboard; I don't want to miss any of this.

"Can I suck you again now?" she asks, her eyes hiding from mine slightly, her face blushed with a pink hue.

"Later. Climb up on top of me and let me inside, Faith."

"Titan—"

"I need inside of you, wife." The word 'wife' slips from my tongue with ease and a sweetness like aged wine. It feels right and that's another thing I'm not going to think about. Not right now. She moves her body and I help pull her up until she's over my cock —exactly where I need her. I encircle her hand in mine and pull it down to my cock, wrapping it around my shaft. "Take me inside," I growl and she doesn't bother to hide the pleasure those words give her. Fuck, her face lights up with pleasure. My cock pulsates at her touch. She guides me to her entrance and she's so wet I feel her juices against my head already. All that wetness... all that excitement from nothing more than sucking me.

Faith Lucas might be fucking perfection.

When she lowers down on my cock, agonizingly slow—I'm sure of it.

"God... I've missed you, Titan," she whispers. Her voice is soft and full of an honesty you can hear. An honesty that shakes me to the fucking core. "You feel so good. It's like heaven when you're inside of me," she moans as she settles on top of me, stretching up to kiss me and causing my cock to scrape against her inside walls, and fuck if that doesn't feel even better.

I take her lips with a hunger so violent the kiss may bruise her lips and I don't care. I need more. My tongue invades her mouth, tearing into her like a soldier ready to conquer. Faith begins riding me, using my cock to bring us both where we need to be. We kiss until both of us are oxygen starved. Her gasp of air vibrates in my ears as I kiss down her throat and then bite into the side of her neck. Again, I don't do that gently. I'm too hungry for her, too starved. My fingers wrap painfully in her hair, only tightening when she rides me harder. I move from her throat, holding her hair so she can't leave me—not that she would, but I'm beyond thinking. My balls are heavy; my body feels as if liquid heat is being poured through it. I'm that damn close to coming.

I lie there and watch as Faith takes what she needs. Her tits bounce up and down—taunting me with her ride. My cock tunnels in and out of her pussy and I watch that too. Her fingers are biting into my sides, scoring the skin as she braces herself. She doesn't ride me gently. She's a hellcat determined to get what she wants and I love that too.

"Titan... Titan..." She whispers my name over and over, and I can feel her tighten against my cock, milking it as her juices rain over my shaft.

Fucking unbelievably beautiful.

"Come for me, Faith. Come for me," I urge her, my fingers moving down to where we're joined. I use the pads of them to rub against her swollen clit. It's thumping against my fingers and so wet it's hard to do anything other than rub and push against it—but then, that's all it takes.

Faith detonates, letting out my name in a long, winding wail of a sound that is loud enough I'm sure they hear it in the next hotel room over and I don't give a fuck. She's bearing down on my cock so hard that my body jerks up and at her tortured, breathy voice I go over the edge with her.

"I've missed you," she whispers close to my ear as I fill her full of my cum. "I've missed you."

My eyes close and I surrender to this woman... to my... *wife.*

Fuck, marrying her might have been the smartest thing I've ever done.

23

FAITH

I look at my signature on the annulment papers and I hate it. I hate everything about it, but I know it's what I need to do. I drop the pen on top of the paper and close my eyes, because this is final and it's painful. It doesn't make sense that it hurts so much—but it does.

I stand and walk back to the foot of the bed and look at Titan sleeping. I thought before he just slept hard because of all of the alcohol in his system. I was wrong. Titan sleeps like the fucking dead, and somehow it's cute. It hurts to move, but it's a delicious ache. Titan used my body so many times and in so many ways last night, I know I'll be sore for days—and I like it.

I don't want to leave—not really, but I decided last night that I need to let go and finally get my life in order. I don't have much money saved up, just what's left from the money I made in Buck-Stop. That's going quick, because my Jeep isn't exactly great on gas. That means I need to make some important decisions quick. The main one is where I'm going next.

There's a few choices, but with money being like it is, the best choice is Texas. Aunt Ida Sue invited me out when I talked to her on the phone yesterday. I think she was secretly hoping Titan would follow me there. With me signing the annulment papers, that's not going to happen. Titan gets what he wants and I got...

Laid. I got laid.

Might as well call a spade a spade.

He is going to wonder about me being pregnant, though, which is why I left him a note beside the signed papers. He needs to know he's in the clear. I gave him my Aunt Ida Sue's address and asked him to mail the papers there too, once they're filed. He's completely free to marry again. I ignore the pain that causes. I don't want to think about Titan marrying anyone. With a sigh, I grab my bag, sunglasses and keys. Then I close the door as gently and as quietly as I can. I thought about waking Titan up, but we said all there was to say between us last night.

The morning sun is already bright and the heat is bearing down as I walk across the parking lot. If I hurry, I can hit Texas by the end of the day—well, if my penny cooperates. I swear there were times yesterday I just went in circles. I'm going to have to change the damn thing if today starts like that. Maybe I should flip a dime this time, kind of change it up and hopefully change my luck.

I hop in my Jeep and start the ignition. I look at the main road and back to the hotel. I stare at the door of the room, trying to will it open.

Nothing happens.

I didn't really expect it to, but a girl can hope.

I pull to the edge of the hotel entrance and stare at the highway. I grab the penny and throw it up. I watch as it flips in mid-air and then lands on the passenger seat with a soft thud.

Tails.

Was that left or right? For the life of me, I can't remember. Today it's right. I reach over and turn on the radio. It's time; time to leave Titan behind me. So I do.

I leave him in a cloud of dust behind my old Jeep and ZZ Top singing about the tube snake boogie. I also do it with more than a little sadness.

But I ignore that.

24

TITAN

Son of a bitch.

I should be used to waking up alone after sex with Faith. I don't know why I thought it would be any different, but for some stupid-ass reason I thought it would be. The room is completely empty, though; Faith's clothes are gone. I grab my slacks, pulling them on but not bothering to button them. They lie low on my hips, but mostly they hide my cock, which is all that's important. When I open the motel's door it doesn't surprise me that Faith's Jeep is gone.

I step back and slam the door so hard the walls of the room shake. I feel like ripping the door off the damn hinges, but I don't.

What is it with this girl and running away from me?

I move back into the room, preparing myself to chase after her yet again. This time I won't take any bullshit excuses. This time she'll sign the annulment papers and once that's done I won't have to see her again. Which is fine, more than fine. Sex last night was good, and yeah, maybe it was the best I've ever had. Still, there's not a woman alive worth this bullshit and I have plans—dreams to start making a reality.

I jump in the shower and ignore the memories of Faith in the shower with me. They immediately spring to mind, but eventually they will fade. I forcefully push them away and shower the smell of the blond demon off of my body.

I thought the two of us turned a corner last night. I don't know what corner it was, but I know I'm pissed that she's run away yet again. Who the fuck does that kind of shit? Hell, as mad as I am right now—and that's fuming—I can still hear her sweetly whispered words.

I missed you.

I turn the water off, ignoring the fine tremor that runs through my hand.

God, I've missed you, Titan.

With every word I remember, every breathy sound of her voice —I get more pissed.

I stomp out into the other room, drying off, and thinking of all the ways I'll punish Faith when I catch up to her. If some of those ways include bending her over the bed and slapping her ass, while slamming balls deep inside of her—well, I ignore those too.

I have my clothes back on and that's when I see them. On the table by the window. I walk slowly, suddenly not in a hurry to see them but knowing I have to. The annulment papers have Faith's signature in big cursive letters and a heart dotting the letter "I". For some reason that makes me smile, when it's the last thing I feel like doing. Beside it I see she's scribbled a note on the back of the envelope I've been keeping the papers in.

I grab it and it's fucking twisted, but I grab it like a man finding water when he's dying for thirst. I don't know how I got so twisted up over a woman so quickly—but damn it... *I am.*

Big Daddy,

I've been a bitch with a capital B, and that's not been fair to you. It's not your fault that I'm a moron and feel like that by the time I'm twenty-six I should be more put together than a wedding that didn't even last twenty-four hours. I don't know why signing these make me feel like a bigger failure at this thing called life, but hey that's not exactly your problem. You have plans and they might be fucked up plans, but still that's more than I have, so I decided to cut you some slack. Happy annulment, hubby. May you get back to enjoying single life soon. Please don't worry about me being pregnant. I've already had my visit from Aunt Flo since Vegas and honestly, I'm on birth control.

I'm going to be hanging out at my Aunt Ida Sue's for a bit. If you could send the final annulment papers there, I'd appreciate it.

Stay cool, Titan.

Your annoying soon to be ex-wife.

Faith

I read the note and frown. I turn it over and Ida Sue's address is scribbled on it. Faith's saying goodbye. She's saying goodbye and giving me what I need to move on. I should be happy.

I wish I knew why I'm not...

25

FAITH

"Well, if it ain't mopey drawers," Ida Sue complains, taking the rocking chair beside me. I could pretend she's not talking to me, but there's no point. I look over at my aunt, taking her in. She has soft brown hair that falls around her head in a long bob cut. It used to be shorter, but over the past year she's let it grow out. She's got sparkling green eyes and despite her age she could pass for forty—which she is not. God, I hope I inherited my father's genes and age that well.

"Well, if it ain't Sponge Bob Smart Ass Pants," I grumble, turning my gaze out to the yard. I don't want to see Ida Sue's you-know-better face. I'd rather stare as Hamburger chases his tail. I've never seen a cow chase its tail before and it's kind of interesting—especially when the damn thing gets dizzy.

"That don't make a lick of sense. Then again, most of the crap you've been doing doesn't."

I close my eyes. Aunt Ida Sue is starting to sound like my sister Hope and I really can't handle that.

"Can we not start the day off with another lecture?" I ask her, knowing it will definitely end up in another lecture.

"Maybe we could if you'd quit using the brains from your mother's side of the family to work with."

"My mother didn't have any brains," I mutter.

"My point exactly. There's Lucas blood in there somewhere. You best start using it before you ruin your life."

"You're sounding just like my sister. So I got drunk and married a stranger in Vegas. I signed the annulment papers. I'm no longer Titan Marsh's wife. Mistake fixed and erased from the history books. No life-ruining shit can spread further," I tell her, my eyes closed as the wave of pain hits. It doesn't make sense, but I liked being married to Titan.

I've been at Aunt Ida Sue's for a month and a half now, and each day not seeing Titan has been painful. There was a part of me that thought he would follow me here. Chase me down and tear up the annulment papers and tell me he wanted to try staying married. It was crazy, but the thought—*the hope*—was there and it hurt when he didn't show. Then two weeks ago, I got the papers in the mail. An announcement that I had been "annulled." The papers didn't come from Titan; they came from a law firm in California instead. When I told Hope, her whispered "Thank God" was like a punch to the gut. I haven't talked to her since. I was about to tell her how much I really liked Titan and how I thought we could have been good together. Her snide remark stopped me from sharing my views. Her comment of: *"You really have screwed up in the past, Faith. Your ex was proof of that, but getting married to Titan? God, Faith, that tops them all."* pretty much ended all conversations. I did remind her at least I didn't lie to my husband and convince him we were married when we weren't—right before I hung up and proceeded ignoring her attempts to call back.

I'm so sick of being viewed as Faith the Screw-up by my sisters. Neither one of them have great track records, but they conveniently forget that. Hope is all happy and she and Aden are so in love they stink of it now, but it wasn't exactly a great start between the two of them and I'm kind of tired of Hope being a bitch about it all.

"Are you hearing me, Faith Lucas?"

I let out a deep, frustrated breath. I didn't hear her, mostly because I was blocking her out and being depressed. Which is apparently something my aunt doesn't like. I really need to find a place of my own. When Ida Sue offered me Petal's old room for free it seemed like the perfect answer.

Boy, was I wrong.

"Don't you breathe like that to me, young lady. You might not be from my loins, but you're my blood."

"Ida Sue—"

"And I reckon being from my blood means I can slap the stupid right out of you since my brother can't. That means I'll be slapping you for a damn long time, because your brand of stupid seems to taking over. So you might want to prepare."

"I told you the problem is all fixed now," I all but growl.

"Bull hockey. Is that fine piece of Godiva chocolate sitting here beside my Faith, making me—*her*—smile?"

"What?" I ask, confused. "Of course not."

"Then it most certainly is *not* fixed."

"But... He's getting married. He had plans. He was just drunk when we got married, Ida Sue," I tell her, whispering the words and ignoring the pain they cause.

"Big deal. Hell, Hope's man didn't know who he was when she grabbed him. That didn't stop her. Men are like making meatloaf, Faith."

"Making meatloaf?" I question—almost afraid to ask. With my aunt you never know what she will say next.

"Exactly that. They have all the ingredients buried in there. But it's not finished. You got to use your hands to squish them up and make them look like you want and add the little small things that give them flavor," she says and I blink. What she says actually makes sense. Not that any of it matters, because it's all finished now. So I just don't say anything. "Of course you have to make sure that when you're finished with them they're not the kind of man that actually lets their *meat* loaf. That's unacceptable. There's too many vitamins and herbs that can fix a limp dick these days. Why, when it comes to Jansen, I—"

"*Annnnnd* we're done. The day I hear about Jansen and his meatloaf is the day I need to be put away in a padded cell."

"I do like meatloaf," he says, coming around the corner of the house. "Is that what's for supper tonight, lovey?" he asks Ida Sue. He walks over to her rocking chair and leans down to give her a soft kiss.

"God I hope not," Ida Sue grins. "But I am hoping for some meat on that old kitchen table."

"Oh Lord, just shoot me now and put me out of my misery," I whine, scared they're going to start talking about sex—which they usually do.

"Quit being so over dramatic, Faith. What you need to be doing is going upstairs, packing your bag and loading your ass up and going to California to tell that fine-ass man to not give up on you."

"It's too late."

"It ain't over until another woman is sleeping in your man's bed and has him all twisted up in her. Which means you got time, so you need to get hopping. I need that cinnamon swirl back in my life."

"Say what?"

"In your life. I meant your life."

"Cinnamon swirl?"

"Fine, sprinkles of pretty deep brown that spice up your life. Tell me that's not Titan to a '*T*'."

"Ida Sue, I love you, but it's just too late. And besides, Titan didn't want to stay married to me. If he did—he would have."

"Then make him want to," she says like that's so simple.

"How would I do that?"

"For starters, you could tell him about that bun you got baking in your oven."

I stop breathing. I haven't told a soul; I've been afraid to say the words out loud. My hand goes to my stomach and I hold it there.

"Ida—"

"Don't even try to start lying to me, Faith Lucas. You aren't so big that I can't bend you over my knee."

"How did you know?"

"Oh please, you've been kneeling at the altar of the porcelain gods every morning at six, like clockwork."

"I don't know how to tell him."

"My Titan deserves to know he's going to be a daddy."

I let the "my" part of her sentence pass. It almost makes me want to smile.

"What if he doesn't believe me? I told him there was no way I could be pregnant. I was on the best birth control on the market, damn it," I whisper, feeling more than a little lost.

"If he doesn't believe you then you tell him to kiss your Lucas ass, and walk out with your head held high. What you don't do is let him hitch his horse to another woman before you tell him."

"I'll think about it," I answer—knowing I won't be able to think of anything else.

"You do that, but do it packing. Black will be here in about thirty minutes."

"Black?"

"Yeah, precious. He's flying out to California with you. You don't need to be flying alone in your condition."

"But—"

"You better just do it. There's no arguing with my woman when she gets an idea in her head," Jansen tells me and I just look at the two of them.

"I'm not ready to go to California. I need to think about this."

"Think about it on the plane. As it is, you'll barely make it to that big fancy church before Titan says I do."

"What?"

"He's getting married this evening."

"Then it's already too late," I murmur, feeling like the world is coming down around me.

"The hell it is. You're a Lucas. We never let go of our man. Even when that man is an asshole. Ask Petal. She wouldn't give up on Orange and as much as I hate to admit it, she was right about that one."

"His name is Luka, lovey," Jansen reminds her gently.

She shrugs and ignores him. In the time I've been here, Orange is all she calls him.

"You really think Titan would want..."

"You'll never know until you grow a pair and go talk to him," she answers with a shrug. It's not exactly comforting or even confidence building, but when I look at her, I know she's right. Titan deserves to know he's going to be a father. It will be up to him what he does with that information.

"I'll go pack," I tell her, getting up out of the chair.

"That's my girl. Now, when you get back, we need to discuss names."

"Names?" I ask over my shoulder, already heading to the front door.

"For little Titan. A name is very important. Titan is a god among men, so his daughters and sons should be too. I'm thinking Zeus for a boy and maybe Eris if it's a girl."

"Eris?" I ask, standing at the door, waiting to go in.

"Supposedly she's a goddess of chaos. It seemed fitting," she says with a sly grin.

"Lord help us," Jansen says with a chuckle. I close the door on Ida Sue telling him how Eris is a perfectly good name.

I have to pack... and get to California... and see my ex-husband... and his new wife to be... and panic.

Definitely panic.

26

TITAN

"You sure about this?" Gavin asks for like the millionth time.

"Quit busting my ass, man," I growl, not needing this shit. I look down at my watch. Thirty minutes until show time. With every minute that passes, I'm more and more convinced I'm making the wrong decision. Having Gavin here poking at me is not helping.

"I'm just saying marriage is a big fucking step," he says—proof he's not going to zip it up.

"Seems to be working out well for you," I respond.

"I love Casey. I've always loved her."

"What-fucking-ever," I growl. I've got a migraine working its way through me and I don't need more of this crap.

"Faith asked Hope about you the other day." This comes from Aden.

"She did?" I ask, doing my best to sound uninterested.

"Yeah. When Hope told her she was glad you two finally got your divorce, Faith hung up on her."

"It wasn't a divorce, it was an annulment," I answer, refusing to look at him. I don't know why the end of my marriage is a bitter pill to swallow, but it is. I don't like when Aden and Gavin talk about it being a divorce too. That implies that Faith and I were truly together and couldn't wait to get rid of each other. That's not what went down—not really. We weren't ever truly married, not in the real sense of the word. A wedding implies vows in front of a preacher, a big church full of your friends and family.

A day like today.

Except I don't want to give Jacey my vows. I don't want to get married. Before, I had a plan. I would get married, Jacey would get her trust fund, and I'd get my job. We'd live separately but together for a year and then file for a quiet divorce. By then the trust fund would solely be Jacey's even if she ran off with her girlfriend. It wouldn't matter if Daddy Dearest disowned her. And I'd have my job. I wouldn't make my father-in-law pissed either, because how could it be my fault that Jacey preferred a woman to my dick?

It was a simple plan. Besides, even if the last part didn't pan out—after a year I would have proven myself as a general manager. I would have had other offers. I could have left the Turnpikes behind and not blinked.

The only problem is that the closer it gets to acting on this plan, the more I want to just say forget it. What does it matter if I'm coming into the game older than most other coaches? I'm not over the hill yet. I can get a small coaching job and work my way up. I have the ability and the knowledge. I can do it on my own and I can do it... *without selling my soul.* Jacey deserves better and she needs to just lay shit out to her father.

All of these realizations would have been better days before the wedding... not as the piano music begins to play outside while guests find their seats.

"Ida Sue says Faith has been sick," Aden says quietly, dropping yet another bomb.

My body jerks as I fight my reaction to that. Of course she's sick. She practically stayed naked the entire time she lived in Colorado and they keep talking about the flu season on the damn news. The girl needs a keeper. There was a time I thought about volunteering for the job, but then she walked out on me again. Hell, there's only so many fucking times a man can stand that.

"That's too bad. She should go to a doctor," I answer, trying to sound unconcerned. I glance at my watch again and my hand tightens into a fist.

Time's running out.

Am I really going to go through with this?

"You don't care?" Aden asks. "You have no feelings about Faith at all?"

"I barely know the bitch." I hide the flinch I make when I call Faith a bitch. She's not. She's funny as fuck, she's smart, sweet and she... *God, she's fucking beautiful.*

I miss her. I miss her so much I ache and it doesn't make sense. In fact, it probably makes me the stupidest fuck in the history of the world, but it's true.

I don't want to do this.

Things with Faith might be over, but I can't make life decisions like I'm making. It's time to man up.

"Just wanted to clear that up, because she's in California."

"She's what?" I ask, Aden's words stopping me from opening the door to the main chapel.

"She's coming in with her cousin Black today. At least that's what Ida Sue told Hope."

"Why?"

"No idea. Maybe she wanted to see her ex-husband get married," Aden says and my gut twists at the thought of Faith being out in the crowd when I give vows to another woman.

Fuck.

"Hey, where you going? We don't go outside until they start the pre-march music," Gavin yells as I open the door. I planned on going to talk to Jacey in private, but the moment I open up the door the music begins.

My time has run out. The only chance I'm going to get to see Jacey is at the altar.

Fucking hell.

27

FAITH

"Black, I don't think this is a smart idea."

"Did you fly out here just to chicken out, Faith?"

"What? No... *Maybe.*"

"That doesn't sound like the Faith I know," he laughs and I roll my eyes at him.

"I mean, how melodramatic can I get? I show up at a man's wedding to tell him I'm pregnant? What if he..."

"He what?"

"What if he has me arrested? Escorted off the premises? Tries to kill me?"

"Of those three, the only possible scenario is escorting you off the premises and if he does that, then what does it matter? You've told him your news and your conscience is clear."

"He could murderize me."

"Murderize?"

"It's a mixture of pulverize and murder. Never experienced it—but I'm thinking it's painful. I really don't like pain, Black."

"It will be fine. I'll be right beside you the whole time," he says and I look up at him for reassurance.

"You really think I need to do this? Can't I just send him a note?"

"If it were me, I'd want to know before I married another woman," Black says, point blank.

I sigh, because I know he's right. That doesn't mean that when Black pulls our rental car into the church parking lot I rush to get out. I look around the gigantic church and my stomach lurches like I'm going to be sick.

"So we're saying if you were getting married you'd want someone you had a one-night stand with—for argument's sake we'll say it's the new mayor's girl Laney—that she's pregnant."

"Fuck, don't even joke about that shit. And quit throwing Laney into anything. That woman's nose is so far up in the air she can smell the clouds."

"She is a little... *uptight*."

"There's the understatement of the year."

"Okay, a lot uptight," I whisper, almost smiling—despite my nerves. Black grabs my hand and squeezes it.

"Stop distracting me with rich bitch snobs."

"Ouch, that's harsh."

"I was trying to be nice—I had other words. But again, stop distracting me. How about you get out of this car and go tell Titan you're pregnant?"

"Just like that?"

"Just like that."

"You make it sound easy, and we both know it's not. That church is full of people, including a bride to be and all of her rich family and friends. None of these people will like to see me coming."

"Well, if you don't get a move on, it will be after they say I do, and trust me, they will like you much less then."

I look at him and close my eyes. My hand goes to the door and I do my best to get my nerves under control.

"Time to go crash a wedding," I whisper, my voice literally shaking.

"That's the spirit," Black says, sounding way too cheerful. I ignore him. I have enough on my plate just concentrating on walking without my legs giving out.

I get to the entrance and I swear it feels like my heart is about to jump out of my chest. I open the big heavy entry doors, wincing at the squeaking sound that seems unnaturally loud. I'm ready to run back outside and forget this whole thing when I feel Black behind me, his hand on my back holding me steady, but also not allowing me to turn around.

The bastard.

I walk through the vestibule, my palms sweating. I look down at my jeans and yellow T-shirt that proclaims my love of waffles and wonder if maybe I should have tried to dress a little better before crashing a wedding.

Why didn't someone point out that I looked like a homeless man?

I swallow down bile trying to rise. Right now would not be a good time to get sick. My hand goes to my stomach and I close my eyes. I just have to tell Titan what I need him to know and then sneak back out before the wedding starts. That seems simple enough.

I go into the main chapel and my heart drops to my feet. There will be no talking to Titan before the wedding. That's impossible now.

The wedding has started and the preacher has already started talking.

Shit.

28

TITAN

"… We are gathered here today to join…"

"Uh… I need a word." I finally say the words, getting them out way too late, but shit… at least I got them out.

"What?" the preacher says, clearly surprised, and I can't say as I blame him. I'd venture to say this shit doesn't happen often.

"Jacey, I think you and I should talk," I tell her and you can hear the gasps throughout the church.

"Nothing like timing." This comes from Aden and I'd cock-punch him, but I've kind of got my hands full at the moment.

"What the hell is going on here, Marsh?" Meyers—Jacey's father—growls, standing up and coming toward us.

"I think whatever is going on is between me and Jacey," I tell him, but even before I say it, I know it's not going to go over well. A moment later, that's proven when Meyers hits me. I wasn't expecting it. I probably should have, but I thought it being a church, and because of what was going on, he would give me time to explain. But I go down like a chump, because her father might be getting up there in years, but he spent his life playing football and he hits like a man who has spent his life pumping iron—because he has.

"Titan!" I hear a scream from the back of the church. Then I hear running. My heart is hammering here, because I know that voice. Fuck, I've been dreaming about that voice. I look up just in time to see Faith pushing Meyers out of the way to get to me.

"What in the fuck is going on here?"

"Daddy, your language!" Jacey yells. "I'm sorry, Reverend," she adds, and that just seems to make her old man angrier.

"I'm not. I want to know what in the hell is going on and who *you* are," he says, looking at Faith.

"I'd like to know that too," Jacey answers.

"This is my wife," I growl, standing up and pulling Faith behind me.

"Your wife?" Jacey and her father question in unison. One's voice is curious, the other is full of even more anger than before.

"Ex-wife really," Faith answers, peeking over my shoulder.

"You've been married?" Meyers growls and he pulls his arm back again. I'm not about to take another hit from him. Jacey grabs his arm, though, and holds him back.

"Not really. We weren't," Faith says again and I frown down at her.

"We were too."

"Well, I mean we were but we weren't."

"Woman, we *were*."

"We got an annulment. Actually, Titan hunted me down to get me to sign the papers so he wouldn't disappoint you," Faith tells Jacey, and for some reason I want to pull her over my shoulder and carry her the fuck out of here, then maybe spank her ass.

"You're saying you two didn't sleep together, then? Why did you get married in the first place?" Meyers asks.

"We—" I start, but again Faith butts in.

"Were drunk," she says, and I definitely want to spank her ass now.

"What in the hell, Titan? I'll destroy you!" Meyers threatens.

"It's fine. Daddy, it's fine. Let's just get this done," Jacey says and guilt hits me. She doesn't care about me, she has her own reasons for this marriage, but I'm about to fuck that up for her.

"About that..." I start, but I needn't worry because Faith pipes in again.

"Could I just talk to Big Daddy one little momento? It's kind of important," she says and I hold my head down and pinch my nose.

"Big... *Daddy*?" Jacey whispers the words, but her father nearly screams them.

"Titan, I really need to talk to you..." she says and I think I see fear in her face.

"Jacey—"

"You leave anywhere with this—"

"I'd be careful what you call my cousin," a guy yells from a few feet away. I've met him before. I think he's White's brother.

"Go talk to her, Titan. You and I can talk after," Jacey responds and I see the recognition on her face. I nod my head in agreement and then turn to Faith, wrap my hand around her upper arm and pull her into the room where Aden, Gavin and I got ready earlier.

Thinking about them, I look over and they're both standing there grinning like fucking fools. After I spank Faith's ass, I may punch them for fun.

FAITH

"Hi," I tell him lamely after he closes the door. It's stupid, but I had to say something. He just keeps standing there, staring at me with his arms crossed as if daring me to move. "You're looking good," I add, because apparently I have a knack for being stupid.

"Why are you here, Faith?"

"Uh..."

"Because if I remember correctly you fucked my brains out and then left me *again*. I kind of took that to mean whatever we had was done."

"Uh..."

"And if that didn't clue me in, the fact that you signed the annulment papers and left me a nice little note sure as hell did."

"Uh..."

"Not to mention that it has been—"

"Will you let me talk?"

"Get to talking," he growls and I'd like to throw something at him, but I don't figure that would be the smart play to make right now.

"I uh... Are you really getting married?" I ask, unable to tell him what I need to and instead asking the one thing that has been bothering me since I found out.

"You got to be shitting me right now," he growls and I bite my lip.

Yeah, I shouldn't have asked that.

"That's probably none of my business," I tell him with a sigh and sit down in a chair, trying to figure out how to get the words out that I need to tell him. Words I don't really want to say.

"Gee, woman. Do you think?"

"I think I liked it better when you called me wife," I grumble.

"But you aren't anymore. You signed the papers."

"You don't get to sound angry about that, Titan. You're the guy who chased me down to get me to sign them. *Remember*?"

"So to be clear, we're saying you came all the way to California to bust my balls?"

"No... I had something to tell you. I was going to write you a letter, but my aunt said it was something you would want to know right away, and that you were getting married. That's quick moving, by the way. I mean, I know you said it was a business deal and all that, but couldn't the ink get a little dry on our annulment before you say I do?"

"Faith," he says, his voice full of warning.

"Okay, fine! I lied to you," I tell him while wringing my hands. My nerves are about to get the best of me.

"You what?"

"I lied to you."

"When... what about? Start talking, woman," he growls and I bite my lip and watch him. I figure the worst case scenario here is that he tries to kill me. My cousin Black is in the next room and my brother-in-law Aden was out there. That probably means Hope is around somewhere. Surely, between the three of them they won't let me die.

"Okay, so it's time to be straight with you," I tell him, trying to sort it all out in my brain.

"Fuck, I'm waiting to see this miracle before I get my hopes up," he says.

"You're not exactly helping me over there. In case you couldn't tell, this isn't easy for me and you being Mr. Pissy Pants is making it worse."

"Mr. Pissy Pants?"

"If the Depends fits you should wear them."

"You're as fucking looney tunes as your aunt with the cow."

"That's not nice—"

"I—"

"—though probably true," I continue, ignoring his interruption. "I mean... I think it's pretty clear."

"I wish to God I could say that," he growls.

"What kind of sane woman leaves a really bad relationship—and when I say bad I mean *really* bad—to end up married by Elvis in an all-night wedding chapel in Vegas? Right? She would have to be insane. You could have claimed that on your annulment papers and I wouldn't have had to sign them."

"Faith, no offense, woman, but I got a man outside who probably is gunning for my life. A fiancée that I may not have feelings for, but the two of us had a deal and you are causing waves in that deal, so I need to talk to her. There's a preacher outside, a room full of people and most of those are *not* my people. All of this means we need to get a move on with this conversation. So can you try to stay focused and give me what you needed to give me, so I can go out and see to shit I need to see to?"

"You could go talk to them first if you want. You and I could have our talk afterwards. Now that I think about it, that might be for the best. It will give me more time to figure out what I want to say."

"Jesus. Woman, just tell me. What the fuck did you lie to me about and why does it even matter now that we're divorced?"

"Technically we're annulled."

"Faith—"

"Okay fine! I lied when I said there was no way I could be pregnant. I mean, I thought there wasn't. I was on birth control. But, I guess… maybe… Somehow it didn't work."

"What the fuck are you saying?" he says and he's a man of color and that color is gorgeous, but I'm pretty sure it's much paler than normal right now.

"Titan… I'm pregnant," I tell him, and I say the words avoiding his face, but when he doesn't reply, I can't resist looking up.

His face is filled with shock and anger… That's definite anger I see.

Shit. This isn't going to go good at all. I'm going to kill my aunt and Black!

Well, if I survive Titan.

30

FAITH

"Are you okay?" Hope asks again, for like the hundredth time. I haven't really answered her once yet. I guess out of all the reactions I imagined from Titan, I wasn't prepared for... *Silence.*

"He... didn't say anything to me," I whisper, admitting the truth that has my stomach in knots.

"It's going to be okay, Faith. I promise it will be," Hope says and then she does something that I love, something that rarely happens, because we were never taught to be that way. She wraps her arms around me and pulls my head to her chest and lets me cry.

That's the exact moment I realize it too. I'm crying. I have no idea how long I've been crying; it might be since Titan stared at me and then turned and walked away without a word. It might have been when Aden, Black and Gavin came in the room without Titan and gently got me out of the church. They were sweet, their faces troubled and they ushered me through the back—away from the crowd.

"Did he get married?" I ask, letting the tears fall and deciding it's okay to be weak at least once.

"No, honey. He called the wedding off. Aden says he was about to before you came to the church."

"Oh... You're right, Hope. I am a screw-up," I confess, lying back on the bed, suddenly feeling exhausted.

"You are not," Hopes argues, and she does it lying back on the bed too. That's when a memory pops up of the three of us sisters hugging on Hope's small bed during a really bad storm. Mom and Dad were fighting—as they often did—and the thunder and lightning was kind of terrifying, especially for three young girls. I don't know when we lost that closeness we used to have—but I will admit I've missed it.

"I married my one-night stand and..."

"*And*... you're going to have a beautiful baby," Hope interrupts me.

"I might be a little scared. I know next to nothing about kids. Mom wasn't exactly a great teacher."

"Faith—"

"I'm going to ruin this baby's life, Hope!" I cry and let my sobs take me over.

"You are not. We had the same mom, didn't we?"

"Yeah," I sniffle into her body and I love my sister, but I really wish it was Titan's arms around me right now. Titan reassuring me that he doesn't hate me and that he loves... that he will love our baby.

"Jack isn't ruined..."

"He's beautiful," I agree because my nephew is. He's the best and he never fails to make me smile.

"And your child will be all that and more to you, Faith," she whispers, kissing the top of my head.

"He walked away without a word, Hope," I tell her again, because Titan's reaction cut me deeply. I was afraid he'd be mad and want to kill me. Now, I realize, I'd rather that had been his reaction. At least, I would have known how he felt...

"It will be okay, sweetheart. I promise. It will work out. You weren't here, you didn't see how destroyed I was when Aden left me, but it worked out. We found our way back to one another. And..."

"You two loved each other. Titan and I are just... fuck buddies," I tell her, and I hate those words. I hate them. Besides, they're not even true. We were a drunken mistake. A mistake that made a child...

"It will be okay. If Titan doesn't man up, you don't need him. You have your family and what's more important, this child has your family and he or she will have you as a mom."

"That's what I'm—"

"And you will be an awesome mother, Faith. You may not believe that, but I definitely do."

I let her words wash over me and I pray she's right.

I'm scared she's wrong.

31

TITAN

"Faith."

I call to her standing in the middle of LAX. She's with Black, and I hate that I've waited this long to talk to her. I didn't really expect her to leave so quickly. I thought she would stay here and visit with Hope. They've moved here permanently while Aden works on the new film he's directing. When I showed up this morning Hope chewed my ass out. It was deserved, I know, so I took it without comment. I had to have a few days to wrap my head around everything. I never planned on becoming a father. I really never planned on it with a woman I'm not in a relationship with. I don't even know how to classify Faith. She's not a girlfriend, she's not even a friend at this point. If anything, she's been a pain in my ass.

And really damn good in bed.

None of that screams relationship. None of that screams mother of my children. So I took a few days to get my head together. I should have known she wouldn't wait around—she never does.

"Titan," she says, her face closed off and the light in her eyes so dull that she looks like a different person.

"We need to talk."

She frowns. Her gaze moves over my body, her face giving nothing away. She looks up at Black and some kind of silent communication moves between them. He nods, then cuts me a look like he'd like to have his own talk with me. I have no doubt he will at some point.

"Titan, they will be boarding the plane soon," she says, her voice somber and without any of the sass that's normally attached.

"Stay here."

"I need to get back. I start a new job next week and I need to find a place to live. Living with my aunt isn't going to cut it with a baby on the way," she says, her pale face coloring with her words like she's embarrassed.

I reach behind the base of my spine and rub the tension that's there, feeling like I'm walking on eggshells. I feel like one wrong step and she's going to completely pull away from me.

"You could stay here—with me, I mean," I respond. I see surprise on her face for the briefest of seconds, before she taps it down.

"I don't think that would be a wise thing to do."

"Why not? It will give us both time to come to terms with what's happening."

"Come to terms? It's not a death sentence, Titan. No one has been diagnosed with cancer or some other kind of disease. It's a baby. My baby."

"Our baby, Faith."

"Only if you want it to be," she murmurs, rubbing her stomach gently.

"What are you saying?"

"I'm just... Look, if you want to be part of this child's life, that's awesome. We can work together and make that happen. But, if you don't, that's fine too. This doesn't have to change anything for you."

"You're pregnant with my child, Faith. That changes everything."

"It doesn't have to."

"It does. Is that what you think of me, Faith? That I'm not man enough to stand up to my mistakes?" I growl and I can't keep the anger from bleeding through. People are starting to gather around us, listening—but, fuck... She wanted to talk here and if that's the only play I have, I'll take it.

"My child is not a mistake," she growls back and she looks ferocious doing it, reminding me of a mama bear protecting her cub. I like it. I like seeing that from her, especially when talking about a child I fathered.

I fathered.

Fuck me if I'm not still getting used to that.

"It's *our* child and I didn't mean it was a mistake, not like that. Shit, woman. Cut me some slack here. You storm into a church and throw this at me. I need a little time to get my head straight."

"You can take all the time you need, Titan. No one is pressuring you to do anything. I'm not asking for one thing from you. I just... My aunt said you needed to know what was going on and she was right. I came here to tell you and I told you."

"So now you're leaving?"

"I have to get back to Texas. I want my child to grow up surrounded by family. That can happen in Texas."

"It could happen here. I'm here. Aden, Hope and Jack are here. Our child would have family."

"Aden and Hope travel more than they stay home. Besides, I like Texas."

"I thought you wanted to go to Arkansas," I remind her, remembering our earlier conversations and giving a weak smile as I think about it. It seems like forever ago now.

"Things change." The intercom announces the boarding of the next plane and Faith holds up her ticket with a sad smile on her face. "I've got to go, Titan. You have my address if you need in touch with me."

"You're leaving? Just like that?"

"Just like that," she answers and walks away.

I let her go. There's nothing more I can do here, but Faith hasn't seen the last of me.

Not by a long shot.

32

FAITH

"I need a ceiling fan above the table. Don't you think, dear?" Ida Sue asks me as I come into the kitchen.

I yawn, looking up at the ceiling. I've been back in Texas a week, and I'm finally feeling like I'm getting control of my life again. I even have an appointment to look at an apartment today. I started work yesterday. I'm a secretary at the local elementary school. It's not a glamorous job, it's even a little boring. But I'm starting to think boring is just fine.

"It would look good up there. Why do you want a ceiling fan there, though? You have that killer light that Jansen made you," I ask. She does. It's a light that I've seen in magazines for big bucks. It's made out of antlers and Jansen put a gloss on them so they shine. It's very rustic and matches Ida Sue's dining room perfectly. It's not my taste, but definitely cool—plus, her man made it for her and that has to mean more than some out-of-the-store ceiling fan.

"This old table gets a lot of use. Hot is good and sweat too, because it means you're working hard and enjoying it, but when you're already sweating it's a little too damn hot to enjoy the things that make you sweat more—no matter how fun. I'm thinking a fan would be good for those days. Not to mention having the wind blowing down... could add a little more to the overall experience."

I blink. I blink again. Suddenly, I think we're not discussing food or having family dinners.

"I'll be late getting in, Ida Sue. I'm going to go by Petal's shop after work. There's an apartment upstairs for rent."

"I still think it's a bad idea. You've had the man calling you since you got here. He gives me a bad feeling."

"He did me too; that's why I left him. I don't know why he's calling now—I left him six months ago. I don't understand, but at least he quit calling."

"Probably because Black threatened to have his buddies in Dallas check into him," Ida Sue murmurs and she's most likely right. He hasn't called since I got back from California though, so I'm taking that as a good sign.

"Yeah," I agree, wondering how my life got so complicated.

"I don't see why you have to move out anyway. Jansen and I love having you here. You've got Petal's room and you can turn little River's old room into a nursery. It's perfect," she says and I can't help the smile I get at her words.

I've never had a real family. My father loved us, but he was struggling with many things—most of those being a woman who owned his heart but liked to grind it into the ground, and she did that often. Aunt Ida Sue always cared about us, but we had distance between us so she couldn't always be there. Our other aunt tried her best to help, but there was only so much she could do because she was a lot older than my father or even Ida Sue. Being here has probably been one of the best times in my life.

I walk over to Ida Sue and hug her, holding her to me. She smells like the blueberry muffins she made for breakfast this morning and that too is something I wish I'd had when I was younger. I can't remember my mother baking anything. I can't remember my mother being in the kitchen—at least not sober.

"I love you," I whisper close to her ear.

"I love you too. Does this mean you're going to make an old woman happy and stay?"

"I can't. I need to stand on my own two feet. I need to make a home for little Zeus or Eris," I laugh.

"There's that Lucas spirit. In that case, I have a key for you."

"A key?"

"Yeah, you don't need to be climbing stairs all the time. Right now it'd be fine, but you give it a few months and that little monkey you're carrying starts dancing on your bladder, then climbing stairs will be the last thing you want to do. This here is a nice three-bedroom house, right down the road from Petal and Orange. Rent is reasonable too."

"Are you ever going to call Luka anything but Orange?"

"Probably not. The things I'm tempted to call him make Petal get all pissy. Besides, those names aren't as fun anymore since I like the big dummy these days."

Her response makes me laugh, but then I look at the key in my hand.

"Whose house is it?"

"A friend of mine. They heard you were staying here and they offered up the house. Check it out, see if you like it and if you do, we can work out the particulars then. I can text you the address."

"Are you sure?"

"Positive."

"I'll do it then. Thank you so much, Ida Sue. I don't know what I'd do without you."

"Well then, you never have to find out, do you? Now, you hurry on along. I need to see what else I can get done around this place besides a fan. Yes-sir-ree, I'm going to get some real spring cleaning done."

"I'll leave you to it, then. Thanks again," I call as I grab a banana and then head out the door. Ida Sue doesn't respond; she's already mumbling about installing something in her bathroom. I'm not sure what, but I could have sworn she mentioned a chocolate fountain. I'm not sure why anyone would want one of those in their bathroom. It seems really unsanitary, but I'm not about to question her.

I'm not that brave.

TITAN

"Did she take the house?" I ask Ida Sue.

The bitch is crazy, even over the phone. Still, she loves her niece and she's helping me take care of Faith. I have to depend on her right now; I don't have a choice. I'm kind of glad we're only doing this over the phone, though. There's some days my ass still hurts from all of her pinching at Aden's wedding.

"She's moving in this weekend. She's expecting to pay rent, though, Tighty. She's not going to be happy when she finds out there is no rent."

"I'll deal with it. And I thought I told you not to call me that anymore." My hand flexes on the phone in irritation.

"That can be arranged if you answer my question."

"Ida Sue—"

"Tighty-whiteys or boxers?"

"I'm not answering that shit."

"So we're talking commando. I like it."

"You are a special kind of Fruit Loops, aren't you?"

"Fine. I have another name for you. It's better."

"I'm dying with anticipation." I laugh, wondering how they let this woman walk the streets alone.

"I just bet you are. When will you be making your appearance in Texas anyway?"

"I have a few more things to close up here. It will probably be next week. Not that it matters. Faith's still not taking my calls." I sigh.

I've made a fucking mess of this. I just can't seem to stop myself. I don't blame Faith for not taking my call. In her shoes, I wouldn't want to talk to me right now. Still, it can't keep going on like this. I'm hoping things go better when I get to Texas. I don't have a lot of hope—but I have to try.

I found that house in a great neighborhood and it's close to some of Faith's family. Luckily, that family is not Ida Sue. I'm not sure I can take being really close to her right now. Which is another reason I'm dreading going to Texas. I get Faith moved into the house, I know I'm going to have to grovel my way back in with her and that means I'll be staying in a motel—there's only one in that small town—or with Ida Sue. None of those options fill me with happiness, but I'll do what I have to. Hopefully, Faith will forgive me sooner rather than later.

"It's the Lucas blood in her. We can be a tad hard-headed," Ida Sue confesses. "She's a smart cookie, though. Once she's sees you're serious, it will get easier."

"I hope so," I answer, rubbing the side of my neck. I don't have a lot of trust in Ida Sue's claim. Nothing with Faith has been easy so far, and I doubt that will magically change.

"It will. You'll see, C.T."

"C.T.?"

"That's you new nickname. Anywho, I have a very important question for you."

"What does C.T. mean?"

"You don't like it?"

"It's better than Tighty," I grumble, closing my eyes. This damn woman could give me a headache.

"Good it's settled then. You'll be C.T. Now about my question..."

"What is it?" I ask, getting tired when she doesn't talk for a bit.

"Do you know how to wire lights?"

"Wire lights?" I repeat, thoroughly confused.

"Yeah, like install a ceiling fan?"

"Well, no, though if it has instructions I can usually figure it out. What does that have to do with anything?"

"Oh, just wondering. Now, to get my part in this 007 plan down, let me recap."

"Okay," I tell her, glancing over at the clock. I've got a meeting with my team GM in an hour. I'm dreading it. Turning in the uniform seems so final, but it's been a long time coming. The job I've managed to grab in Texas isn't my dream job, but I'm kind of looking forward to it. The money is mostly shit, but there's a pension plan, yearly bonuses and the house I've moved Faith into—without her knowing—was supplied in the deal. It's not the money I once made, but then, it won't be the same lifestyle either and I'm okay with that. I'm actually kind of excited about it.

"I get Faith in the house you bought, help her move out of my house. You move in with me for a year—"

"Only if there's no room in the motel and—"

"There won't be," she says, sounding perfectly serious.

"...and I didn't say a year. How do you know about the motel?"

"I... uh... checked today. They're booked up solid for the next month."

"Fuck," I growl, feeling the dream of my own space—and protecting my ass from Ida Sue's fingers—fading away.

"So, you will stay with me for a year and—"

"It won't be that long. I just need to get Faith to forgive me," I argue, praying to God it's nowhere near a year. If Faith can't forgive me and I can't interest her in trying to make the two of us work as a couple, then... Then I'll find a place to rent and I'll be there for my child.

I just hope Faith will let me try to be there for her too.

"Back to the plan. You'll stay with me and work on getting my niece to forgive you. Do I have all that right?"

"Pretty much."

"Okay then, C.T., you best be getting a move on. You got a big mountain to climb and you need to be down here to climb it."

"Okay—"

"Preferably without a shirt on," she says and I can hear the laughter in her voice, but I also hear the eager tone too.

"Just like I said, you're a special kind of Fruit Loop," I tell her, shaking my head. I don't want to like her, but I can't seem to stop myself.

"I prefer Cocoa Puffs. They're just the right shade of chocolate."

"You did not just say that."

"Later, C.T.," she laughs and then the damn woman hangs up.

Christ. I really hope Faith lets me in with her again... *and soon.*

34

FAITH

"I don't understand. How can they *not* charge me rent for the first month?"

"He's got the flu, peach blossom. You want him to drag his ass out here with a fever of 108 to collect your rent?"

"He's got a fever of 108? Shouldn't he be in the hospital?" I ask, not knowing temperatures could even go that high.

"Or the morgue," Black says and I frown.

"Oh my God, I know this sounds horrible, but what if this friend of yours... What was his name again?"

"I call him C.T. His name's kind of a tongue twister."

"What if C.T. dies?!?! I just moved in. I'd hate to lose the house."

"He's not going to die," Ida Sue says, and she really doesn't seem worried. Still, a temperature of 108 seems... *extreme*.

"Unless someone kills him," Black says and I frown at my cousin.

"No one's going to kill him," Ida Sue growls at Black. They stare at each other a minute and I'm pretty sure I'm missing some pertinent information to this conversation.

"You never know. He's not made any friends in this part of the woods. In fact, my brothers and I would like to smash his face in."

"You and your brothers will do no such thing. I forbid it," Ida Sue yells. She does this loudly and there's anger in her words—enough that I take a step back.

"What am I missing here?" I ask, confused.

"C.T. made a few bad decisions," Ida Sue says with a heartfelt sigh.

"That's a freaking understatement," Black says.

"Your cousins are a wee bit upset with some of his recent decisions."

"Another freaking understatement."

"Oh. Should I not rent the house? I could still get the apartment above the beauty shop," I ask, directing my question at Black. I don't want to jump into a huge mess.

"That's crazy talk right there. This house is perfect. The master bedroom and bath are so nice and the small nursery will be great for baby Zeus or Eris," Ida Sue argues. "Plus, Cherry Blossom, look at this yard. Your babies could run and play for days."

I laugh. For the last few days Ida Sue has tried different "blossom" names for me. She's asked to adopt me, even though I keep telling her you can't adopt grown adults. Her response was classic Ida Sue: she said she can adopt me, she just has to find the right name. I don't know what to say to that, other than I love her—which I do, even if she is crazy as hell.

"I don't think I need to worry about the yard. I probably won't be here long enough for the baby to be running—and that's *bay--be*, singular, definitely *not* plural," I laugh.

"Why wouldn't you be? I thought you liked it here."

"Well, I do. It's a great place for a kid to grow up. But I'm renting. I doubt the owner is really looking for any contract to be long term."

"Exactly the reason I want to smash his face in," Black growls.

"What?"

"Nothing. Black forgot to take his fiber medication this morning. It makes him grouchy when he can't poop correctly."

I cringe. That's something I really didn't want to know about my cousin.

"Well, you're right about one thing, Mom. Someone around here is sure full of shit."

"Black Heart Lucas! You need to shut it!"

"I don't have a middle name, Mom."

"You do now! I just added it!"

I know they're arguing, and I'm confused as hell, but I listen to them and giggle.

"I'm going to make sure Faith's water is turned on and her windows are locked," Black answers, walking away, and it's clear he's still angry.

"Wow. He is *really* upset with your friend."

"He is, but he'll get over it. C.T. just needs to prove himself again, and he will."

"What did he do?"

"That's not my story to tell, Ginger Blossom. But I think everyone deserves a second chance, don't you?"

"I never thought about it. I guess so. Unless maybe, murderers and people who harm children and maybe pets. Really, Ida Sue, I can't answer since I don't know what this C.T. did."

"He just made a mistake, Tater Blossom, but it wasn't illegal. Everyone makes mistakes, even my damn boy. One day he'll be eating his words."

"You have that much confidence in your friend?"

"I do, but then there's a lot on the line for him and I've found when a good man is faced with losing everything, he tends to get his head out of his ass pretty quick."

"Well I hope he fixes everything, especially since you seem so fond of him."

"Me too, Turtle Blossom, me too."

"Aunt Ida Sue?"

"Yeah?"

"Let's just call me Blossom..."

She grins really big and I get the feeling she got what she wanted all along. I've agreed to be "adopted" and I didn't even see it coming.

TITAN

I'm so nervous I feel like I'm about to face the firing squad. I rub the side of my face, frowning. I should have shaved this morning. I came here straight from the airport. I thought about going to Faith's looney-tunes aunt first, but sadly... *this* seemed the safer of the two choices.

And if I'm completely honest, I wanted to see Faith again. I haven't laid eyes on her since that day at the airport and I've found the strangest thing happened.

I missed her.

I missed her after she left me with the annulment papers, but she made her choice and it pissed me off at the time, but I decided to move forward. I did that and when it got time to marry Jacey...

I was done. I was going through with the plan, despite knowing I shouldn't. I was going through with the plan at Jacey's urgings... *at Cora's urgings.* I was going through with the plan because I felt lost and the promise of the general manager position might fill that void. But when it came up to that moment, I couldn't do it. Was going to call it off, and then Faith showed.

That was not how I wanted her to see me again. That's all I

processed. I didn't want Faith to see me being a chump, making chump moves—because that's all that was. A play for a fucking job, doing what I was doing—even with Jacey knowing my motives and her having some of her own—was a chump-ass move and that's what Faith saw.

Then came her news.

Pregnant.

I haven't begun to process that. I'm not sure I know how right now. What I do know is I need to make sure Faith is taken care of —preferably by me, but at least so that I'm close enough to know she's okay.

I had a grand scheme to marry a woman I did not know, and barely spoke to. A scheme that came into play at a party when she approached me. I have no grand scheme on what to do with Faith. A woman I know, mostly like—except when I want to throttle her —and a woman who is having my baby.

If I was going to have a plan, right now would sure as hell be the correct time to have it. And I have...

Absolutely nothing.

My attention is brought back to the door; I am just about to knock again when the curtain covering the glass panels move. Faith's eyes find mine and she stares at me for a moment. Somewhere in the back of my mind I make a note to have her front door changed. Half the door is made up of six small glass panels which have been sectioned off in squares by trim. It's cute and matches the feel of the house, but glass breaks and it does that easily. That leaves Faith vulnerable... *Faith and my child.*

Her face tightens, and her eyes dull. She's not happy to see me. I didn't expect she would be, but I had hoped.

"Let me in," I tell her, feeling like an ass, but apparently not able to articulate words that might soften her toward me. Then again, I'm not sure words are invented that might make Faith like me right now.

"What are you doing here, Titan?" she asks, finally opening the door.

I take a minute to just look at her. Faith's blond hair is rumpled from sleep and it's all clipped to the top of her head. She has circles, dark ones, and I don't like them. She's way too pale. Guilt flares up strong inside of me. I should have been here sooner to watch over her. I force myself to look away from her face. My gaze travels to the rest of her body and it's been a while. I could be mistaken, but I think she's lost weight. Faith's pregnant, she shouldn't be losing weight. I take in the faded blue robe she's wearing that is cinched at the waist. A waist which is not swollen with a child, but I know it's coming. Soon her flat stomach will be swollen with my child and something twists inside of me at the knowledge. I never thought about being a father, not sure I ever wanted to be.

Looking at Faith's stomach right now, I'm bombarded with emotions and questions. I'm not ready to sift through them just yet.

"Hi, Faith."

"What are you doing here?" she asks again.

"I was hoping we could talk." That definitely sounds lame. What the fuck has happened to me? Apparently finding out I'm going to be a father has disconnected my brain.

"I don't think we have much to say to each other. At least not until the baby gets here."

"I think you're wrong."

"Ask me if I care what you think," she responds, some of the fire in her eyes returning. I don't really want her angry at me, but at least she's showing some emotion and for some reason that makes me feel better.

"Will you let me in, please? We'll talk. We need to talk—if not for us, for the life you're carrying."

I watch as her hand travels to her stomach. She rubs it gently and my gut tightens. A slow burning heat spreads through my body. She's thinking of the baby... *of our baby*... and it's clear that she cares for the child already. I don't know why that surprises me, but fuck if it doesn't and I can't say I don't like it.

I do. I like the fact that she's pregnant with my child and there's a part of her happy about it. I like it a fuck of a lot.

Maybe because I feel the same...

Shit.

36

FAITH

I open the door wider and wait for Titan to come inside. He had to find me through my Aunt Ida Sue. I may kill her. I know she has a crush on him—in that she wants him to be the new model at her sculpting class she's taking at the Y—the *nude* model. Still, I wasn't ready for Titan to know where I live. I wasn't really prepared to see him just yet. I knew it was coming, but I was all for letting it lie for now. He walks in, and my house has high ceilings and large rooms, but instantly it feels smaller. I ignore that and lead him into the kitchen. If I'm going to have to talk to him, I'm going to need to do that with coffee in my system.

He sits at the bar, looking very uncomfortable, and I won't lie, seeing him like that brings me pleasure.

"Do you want some coffee?" I ask him, giving him my back as I turn to the coffee pot and start putting in the pod and filling it with water.

"Should you be drinking coffee? I mean, you are pregnant. That can't be healthy for the baby."

"And that would be a no," I grumble, ignoring him. I drink decaf and not a lot of that, but I'm not about to start explaining myself to him.

"I'll take a cup," he says quietly.

He's silent after that and we face each other with the sound of the coffee percolating in the background. I lean against my kitchen cabinet, grateful there is a bar between us. He looks good, and I don't want to admit that, but he does. He's wearing jeans—which is something I've not really seen him in. Titan can make suits and dress slacks look really good. He however, makes a pair of Levis fill out so damn good that it hurts to see. He's got on a dusty blue tee that is stretched across his broad muscles and looks soft and somehow sweet against his dark skin. Skin that I've touched, skin that I've missed...

I force my mind away from those thoughts.

"Not today, Satan," I mutter as I turn around to take the cup of coffee that has brewed, and begin going through the motions to do another one. My single cup coffee maker was perfect just for me and I was kind of in love with it, but right now I'm cursing it. If I could get the coffee done and get Titan out of the door—*quickly*—I'd be over the moon with joy.

"What?" he asks, clearly confused. I don't bother to repeat myself or deny what I said. Instead I hand him his cup.

"Do you want sugar? Milk? Creamer?"

"I'm fine," he says, his voice tight.

"What are you doing here, Titan?"

"You're pregnant with my child, Faith."

"I was pregnant when I was in California. You didn't want to talk then," I remind him.

"I tried."

"At the airport, when I was leaving. You had time to do it before that. Your silence spoke volumes and what it spoke was not good, Titan."

"I needed time to process everything. You can't just spring shit on me like that, and expect me to know what to say right off," he argues.

Frustration is etched on his face and maybe I'm being unfair—in fact, I know I am, but I don't care. I hate the words he uses when he talks about my child. I hate the expressions on his face when he looks at me *or* talks about our child. I hate all of it. Most of all I hate that I slept with this guy before I signed his damn annulment papers, and I did it thinking he was a good guy. And if I think on that, the thing I absolutely hate the most is that I thought he was a good guy, because that time in California where he didn't talk to me, I began to realize maybe I was wrong. The time I've been back in Texas and him never reaching out and checking on me—all of that proved to me that I was wrong. So I don't care that I'm not being fair. I don't think I have to be.

"I didn't unload *shit* on you. I told you I was pregnant. I didn't ask for anything from you, Titan. I just thought you'd want to know."

"I did, Faith. Shit, I just wasn't... prepared."

"You think I was?"

"I'm seeing you weren't," he says quietly, but his words don't make me feel better—not at all.

"I wasn't prepared. I was panicked, full blown panicked. But I came to you with my news. It wasn't easy. It took a hell of a lot out of me to do it."

"How long are you going to bust my balls over this? I was at my wedding to another woman. It was an agreement, but it was still a fucking huge wedding."

"Yeah. You didn't let any moss grow under your feet either."

"Why in the hell are you acting like we had something when we didn't? I didn't keep Jacey, the deal or my plans from you, woman. I hunted you down *because* of those plans."

"And then you found me. We may have not had anything before, but after that last night, we might have," I growl back before I can stop myself.

"We had sex, it was really good sex, but I woke up alone. You were gone with those papers signed. That gave me the green light to go ahead with my plans. It might suck to hear it, but it was just sex, Faith. It didn't tie my dick to you."

His words lance through me, searing as they go. I blink and my breath catches, so destructive is that blow. He's right—but he is also not right. So I let him have it. I've been storing it up for weeks, so I have it to give and I think he just earned it. So I give it to him straight.

"Maybe not until that point. We were nothing then, you're right. But that night we weren't drunk, Titan. We were both there in that moment, Big Daddy."

"It was sex and—"

"And I didn't hear you crying, 'Oh no, get off my dick'," I tell him, almost at the point where I've had it with him.

"I'm a man, not like—"

"That's yet to be determined in my eyes."

"I could remind you just how much of a man I am," he answers and that makes me *really* done.

"Get out," I growl.

"Faith—"

"Don't Faith me. Get out. We had sex and I signed your papers. It could have been a new beginning for us. You knew where I was and we could have started over—took things slower. And that's fine, I get that you weren't interested in that. That happens and it sucks since I liked you, but like I said, that's fine. But, what you don't get to do is sit in my kitchen and tell me I'm overreacting, or that it's my fault this all happened and I laid it at your feet. You don't get to do that. So what you need to do is leave."

"We need to talk," he growls again, but he's looking at me differently. Maybe he can tell how deep he cut me, or maybe he's starting to get scared I'm two steps away from kicking him in the dick. Whatever it is, I don't care. I just want him gone.

"You need to leave," I virtually scream. I want him gone; I don't want him breathing my air. I don't want him around my baby's air. Not right now, and maybe never—but definitely not right now.

"I can see you're upset."

"Gee—"

"So I'll leave, but I'm not leaving Texas, Faith. I'm staying and you and I, we're going to talk about this. We're going to talk about it like two rational adults and we're going to come up with a plan."

"I have a plan. I'm raising my child."

"Not without me, Faith. Not without me. I'm going to be a part of my child's life. That means I'm going to be a part of *your* life."

"Will you just leave?" I ask, my voice merely a whisper. I can't deal with him right now. I just can't.

"I'm going... *for now.*"

I don't respond to his warning. I'm not even sure I breathe until he's out the door. I stare at his coffee that he didn't touch. I slide to the floor, staring at that coffee until the image of it dissolves into my tears.

Then... I let myself cry.

37

TITAN

"Hi, Faith."

I watch as her face slowly moves and she looks at me. Those blue eyes, so blue you could get lost in them, focus on me and then her face goes tight. She's not happy to see me, but then I didn't expect her to be.

"What are you doing here, Titan? Are you following me?"

I look around the small park. It's nearly empty; there are just a few people out enjoying the fresh air. I wasn't following her, but I was driving by her house. I wanted to just drive by and make sure everything was okay. I actually wanted to see her, but I knew I couldn't knock on her door—not after our last visit. But I saw her from the road sitting on the bench and I couldn't resist walking over here. I don't want her to know I'm living with her aunt just yet, but I know the day is coming. Ida Sue invited Faith over for dinner tonight, but Faith told her she couldn't make it because the school she's working at was having a basketball game, and Faith was tasked with taking admission at the door. All this means that Faith will be having dinner at Ida Sue's tomorrow. That also means she will soon discover I'm not only staying in town, but that I'm living with her aunt. I'm sure this news won't fill her with happiness, but it has to happen. The one thing I have no idea about... is how to fix this mess. I need Faith to soften toward me. I seem to just keep sticking my foot in my mouth with her over and over. Everything I say comes out wrong.

"I was just out walking and saw you."

"Then maybe you could keep on walking."

"What are you reading?" I ask instead of responding. I motion toward her book.

"Funny you should ask," she says and then holds out the cover to me. I read the words and a smile pulls at my lips.

"How to Survive Stupid Decisions."

"I guess I don't have to ask what your stupid decision was."

"I guess you don't," she agrees.

"What if I started this conversation with I'm sorry I've been such an asshole?" I ask her.

She studies me and I try to remain still during it. I just need to get us back on even ground. There's more here to consider than just me or Faith. *Much more.*

"I'm not sure asshole quite covers it," she finally says and she even manages a small smile. It's the kind of smile that doesn't touch her eyes, but it's there just the same.

"Dickhead?"

"I think you're insulting dickheads everywhere."

"Maybe I could just leave it at I'm sorry for right now?" I suggest.

"I'll think about it. What are you doing here?"

"It's a park. I was clearing my head and saw you." I shrug, giving her the truth, even if it is the bare bones of it.

"I meant in Texas. Shouldn't you have jumped a plane straight back to California? I would have thought when I kicked you out of the house last week you would have left immediately."

"I'm thinking of moving to Texas permanently," I answer. I watch as her eyes dilate, her body tightens and I'm afraid I've pushed it too far again. But whatever she's feeling, she buckles it down and rises above it.

"I thought you guys had to stay close to your team. Don't you have practices and things?"

"I was cut from the team. It was happening before I met you in Vegas and part of the reason my head was in the space it was in," I tell her and then I wince because I realize how that sounded and it's not what I meant. "I didn't mean... Fuck, Faith, I... Help a man out here, will you? I always seem to be putting my foot in my mouth when it comes to you."

Then the strangest thing happens. Faith... *giggles.*

"I got it, Big Daddy. Life had been kicking you in the balls and you got drunk."

"Pretty much. You know, I think I've missed you calling me Big Daddy. Never thought that would happen," I say, shaking my head and sitting on the bench beside her. She tenses, so tightly I can feel it in the air, but she doesn't stand up and leave. So maybe I'm getting somewhere.

"Freak," she mutters.

"You don't seem as angry as you were last week," I tell her, trying to tentatively direct the conversation.

"I've had some time to think things over. I *suppose* you finding out about the baby the *way* you did and *where* you did wasn't ideal."

"You can say that again," I agree, feeling...hope.

"You were still an ass," she grumbles and I don't really have anything to say to that, because I was.

"I want us to be friends, Faith."

"Friends?" she asks, disbelief and maybe shock mingled in her voice.

"Is that so hard to believe? You're having my child. That's a bond between us no matter what our past is."

"Doesn't seem to me, Titan, like you want to be part of this child's life."

"I do. If I didn't I would have never come to Texas, Faith."

"So you're saying we start over? Become..."

"Friends."

"How much of a bitch does it make me if I tell you I'm not sure I want to be friends with you?"

"That just means I'll have to try hard to make you see what I already know."

"What's that?"

"That we'll make great friends."

She doesn't really respond to that and her face is filled with skepticism, but for the first time since I decided to come to Texas I'm feeling a little better about the decision.

I just hope I can prove to her we can be friends. We have to be... because I really want to be a part of my child's life. With every day I spend thinking about it, I'm more and more certain of that.

It's everything else I'm feeling lost with.

38

FAITH

"Good Lord, Ida Sue. It's a thousand degrees in here. What's going on?" I ask, walking through the living room.

I'm not exaggerating either. It's miserable in here. I mean, outside was warm, because this is Texas and the heat has picked today to play with us, but inside Ida Sue's house is a whole other dimension—and that dimension is hell.

"It's hot as Cyan's balls after his all-night sex parties," my cousin Mary growls. Her hair is pushed on top of her head, she's using a paper fan and she's wearing a bikini top and cut-off shorts —all that and she's still sweating like a hooker in church.

I'm starting to rethink wearing my jeans and T-shirt myself.

"Hey, Blossom! I'm in the kitchen!"

Mary barely acknowledges me. As mean as she looks right now, that might be a good thing. Still, before I leave the room she literally growls at me, "This is all your fault, Faith." Then she stomps off.

I have no idea what she means. Mary and I have always gotten along. I shrug it off, thinking the heat just makes her grouchy. I walk into the kitchen, wondering if I can convince Ida Sue we should go out to eat.

"Ida Sue, this heat can't be good for the ba—" I stop when my gaze locks on the scene in front of me. "—by..."

The kitchen table has been pushed off to the side. In the place it usually sits is a ladder and on that ladder is... *Titan.*

"There's my girl. How are you feeling?" Ida Sue asks.

My mouth goes dry. My blood is strumming a loud, wild song in my ears. It's not just the shock of seeing Titan.

"What are you doing here?" I ask, my mouth falling open after I manage to get the words out. Titan is on a ladder working on the chandelier—or rather where it was. He's wearing those tight Levis again, only now he doesn't have a shirt on. He's sweating—because again, it's hotter than hell in here—and the perspiration is running down the sides of his neck. I follow one slow dripping trail as it glides down his shoulder, over his pecs, making a path that leaves me feeling flushed in a way that has nothing to do with the heat in the room. It slinks lower, moving over the indention of each ab so lovingly I wish I could follow it with my tongue.

"Quite a show, ain't it, Blossom?" Ida Sue says with a lecherous grin, elbowing me gently in the side.

I'm really starting to hate the nickname Blossom.

I watch my aunt watch Titan and I know her face mimics what mine was doing just a minute before. It wouldn't surprise me if she didn't start drooling.

"Your aunt's AC broke down and she had a ceiling fan she wanted installed in the kitchen," Titan answers. He looks down at me and gives me a smile that makes butterflies take flight in my stomach, those beautiful eyes of his sparkling, his face almost tender. "You look really good tonight, Faith."

"I... uh... *thanks.* I meant, what are you doing *here?*"

"He's staying with me while he finds a place in town," my aunt answers—ever helpful.

"He's... *Titan?*"

"Didn't have many options, babe. Ida Sue offered, seemed the best solution."

I ignore the way he casually tossed in the word 'babe' and then

I ignore the tingles that run through me when he said it. I try to concentrate on the biggest problem. The one that has the most potential to rock my world off its foundation.

"The best solution... *to what*?"

"I told you I was moving here, Faith. I didn't lie."

Oh crap. I mean, I know he said that, but somewhere in my head it all got fuzzy. I thought he'd get tired of staying and go back to California. Seeing him in my aunt's house—an aunt he complained for weeks about because she kept pinching his ass—does not sound like he's doing something he will give up on. I don't know *what* it says, but it doesn't seem like a good thing for me.

"Titan, aren't you jumping the gun a little bit? I mean, we just found out I'm pregnant. There's no need to make life-altering decisions right now. We can figure it all out when little Zeus or Eris gets here."

"Zeus or Eris?"

"Greek gods. It was my idea, sugar-lumpkins. With a dad named Titan, the baby needed a special name," Ida Sue chirps cheerfully. "Of course we could always continue the family tradition. How do you feel about naming your son Turquoise?"

"Turquoise?"

"Pretty, right? We could call him Turq for short. Turquoise Vegas... or was it Colorado where the soldiers finally swam home, Faith?"

"I think I'll just leave and we can do dinner another night—after the air is fixed," I answer instead, totally ignoring my crazy ass aunt's questions.

"Nonsense. The pizza will be here soon."

"Pizza?"

"I ordered it. There was no way I could cook in this kitchen. But when Titan here gets the fan going, it should cool down enough to eat. I hope you're hungry, I ordered a ton. Once the air stopped working, though, everyone began bailing. White and Kayla couldn't make the trip here, they had a parent-teacher conference, Gray and C.C. are stuck at home with sick babies,

Black refuses to eat dinner with us because I won't let him hit Titan."

"I'd like to see him try," Titan grumbles, stepping down from the ladder. He's got a cloth he's rubbing his hands on as he steps into me, invading my space.

"Why does Black want to hit you?"

"Because I was an insult to dickheads everywhere," he says with a soft smile. I stare at the smile and the way the white of his teeth shines little by little. I stare so long that I have the strangest urge to reach up and kiss those lips, run my tongue over them, lose myself in them. I shake my head.

It's just pregnancy hormones. That's all it is.

"Babe?"

"When did the babe thing start?" I ask, because clearly I've lost my mind. I sound annoyed, because I am. Every time he calls me babe I feel a little shiver run through me.

"What?" he asks, his face moving to show confusion, and I watch every movement. I watch it and enjoy the show, because he's close, because he's beautiful, and because I like it. I watch because I'm insane and I do it while thinking that if this is not pregnancy hormones I'm in deep shit.

"You're calling me babe," I grumble and my frustration shines through and I can tell that bothers him because those soft eyes cloud and the small lines around them tighten.

Yes, I'm staring at him that close.

"Can't really call you wife now, Faith," he points out.

His words are spoken plain and simple. There's no vehemence behind them, no attitude given to indicate he meant to serve a blow—but he did. The words hit me and when they hit... *they hurt.*

They shouldn't have, but they *did*. Still, that isn't his problem and after his last visit I swore to myself I'd stop reacting to Titan emotionally. There is a child involved, a child he obviously wants to play some sort of role with. I grew up with a parent who didn't want a role in my life, and felt like she was forced to do that. It's crazy—especially since she had three kids, but it was true. She didn't want us. We felt that every single day.

Every. Single. Day.

I don't want my child to know that feeling. I never wanted them to. So I swallow down my pride, paste a smile on my face and shrug away the hurt.

"Got it," I say, and maybe my voice is a little tight, but I ignore that and avoid Titan's eyes.

"Does the fan work now?" Ida Sue asks. I hadn't realized she was gone, but she's walking back to us holding a glass. "Here you go, some of my sweet tea to quench that thirst you raised," she adds.

Titan is still looking at me. His gaze is locked on me, and I don't know what he's thinking. He looks thoughtful and his face is almost soft and for some reason I wish I could read his mind; I wish I *did* know.

"Thanks," he mutters, taking the glass from Ida Sue. He takes a few steps away from us, putting some of the tools he used to work with down on the table.

"Oh, it works perfectly! C.T., you're magnificent! Isn't he magnificent, Faith?" she asks.

I should have, but I didn't. I was hot, I was mourning the fact —however stupid it was—that Titan no longer called me "wife," and therefore the initials Ida Sue used floated right past me. Instead I am caught up in the view, because Titan tilts his head back, perspiration still gleaming on his dark skin, and drinks the tea. And when I say that, I mean he tilts the glass up and while he drinks, I watch the way his throat moved, his adams apple teasing as it shifts. Jesus, how a man can be that sexy drinking out of a glass with pink flowers on it is beyond me—but it is true.

"Quite the show, isn't it, Blossom?" Ida Sue asks softly in my ear, repeating her earlier question, and it may be a different show, but the star of it is the same and she's not wrong.

"Damn it, Lovey! Why is it a million degrees in here?" Jansen asks, coming in from the back door, and yanking me out of my Titan haze—*mostly*.

"Our AC broke down," she says, not tearing her eyes away from Titan—not that I blame her. It takes work for me to do it, but I do my best to focus on Jansen. "Titan was nice enough to install a ceiling fan for me. It should cool down soon," she says—again keeping her eyes glued on all that is my ex-husband.

Jansen stalks over to us. He takes one look at a shirtless Titan, one look at a spellbound Ida Sue, and his face goes tight.

"Son of a bitch," he growls under his breath and then he literally *stomps* from the room. I stand there, watching him go—not really understanding. Until a minute later.

"Ida Sue, why the fuck do you have the heat set on ninety-two?" Jansen growls from the hall.

I watch as my aunt is pulled from her Titan-lust-filled haze and annoyance moves over her face.

"That damn man is too smart," she grumbles under her breath, but I still hear it and I can't stop the laugh that bubbles out. Ida Sue goes to the hallway for what I can only imagine is damage control.

Titan is standing to the side and with the shocked look on his face, I laugh harder.

"I got played," he grumbles.

And I laugh even harder.

"Damn it," he growls.

And I laugh so hard, I feel tears seeping from my eyes.

TITAN

"I don't think Jansen is your biggest fan," Faith laughs. We're out on the porch, because even with the air conditioning going full blast in that damn house, it's too hot to breathe. Everyone grabbed their own box of pizza and retreated wherever. I saw Jansen drag crazy Ida out toward the barn. Wouldn't have been my first choice, but they didn't take a pizza box so I figured they weren't really eating.

"Your aunt is crazy as hell," I tell Faith after taking a bite of pizza.

"She's good people though," she says softly, staring up at the sky.

"Yeah, she is," I answer and I'm not talking about her aunt. I clear my throat, because suddenly it's tight.

"Titan—"

"Faith—"

We say the names at the same time and she smiles, her face gentle and kind.

"You first," she prompts.

"No, you go ahead," I tell her, because fuck, I have no idea what I was about to say. I just wanted to keep her here...*with me.*

"I was going to tell you that you didn't have to stay here."

"Are you offering your place?"

"What? *No,* of course not... I didn't mean that."

"Damn, for a minute there I had hope."

She frowns and looks at me. "Titan you don't need to live here at all. You have a life in California and you can still be a part of this child's life even if we don't live in the same state," she says.

I put my pizza back on the box that sits between us. Faith and I are sitting on the top step of the porch. I push it back, out of my way, and move my hand along the side of her neck, holding her face gently.

"I want to be with you when the baby moves. I want to hold your hand when we see the baby for the first time... Hell, I want to be there for each of the doctor's appointments. I want to be the one with you when we find out if we're having a boy or a girl. If I'm completely honest I want a hell of a lot more than that, Faith. I'll bide my time, but I will do it here, because that's where you are, that's where our baby is and that's what matters."

"It's kind of crazy to move and start over, considering we don't know much about each other and we're..."

"We don't know what we are yet, Faith. We're going to find out," I tell her, my eyes dropping down to her lips.

"We are?" she asks, her voice husky.

"Definitely," I tell her and because I can't resist, I bend down to touch her lips. It's a brief kiss that I don't press. It's just lips touching, but it has depth behind it. It has *meaning* behind it—whether she realizes it or not.

"So we're starting over?" she asks when I pull away.

I want to laugh, because starting over means we forget the past and that's not happening. I'm never going to forget how it feels to slide between her legs and sink inside. *I don't want to forget.*

"What?" I ask, giving in to the urge to smile.

"We'll start over. We'll be... *friends.*"

"Friends?" I ask, not really liking the sound of that. I have friends. I don't have the urge to kiss them, to bend them over and bury myself inside of them—but I definitely do with Faith.

"Friends," she says like we're in agreement and she's smiling large...

I'm frowning.

FAITH

"Titan?" I squint at him through sleepy eyes and lean heavily on my front door frame. A smiling Titan is standing on my doorstep, wearing more jeans—these just as sexy—and a red cotton T-shirt. He's holding a white bag and two cups and he looks... *cheerful.*

"Hey, I thought I'd bring you breakfast."

"Breakfast?" I ask, wondering if I'm dreaming. I did dream about Titan last night and maybe I still am. I'm probably not awake at all. It's not daylight and I'm not standing in front of Titan with morning breath, ratty bed hair and wearing pajamas.

"Friends buy each other breakfast, don't they?" he laughs and all hope fades. The Titan in my dreams would not be talking about being friends. He'd be getting busy doing all the things that make me ache—and continue to dream about him.

"It's early," I complain. I look behind me at the clock. It's barely seven thirty in the morning.

"It is, but I know you had work today, so I wanted to catch you early. I actually meant to make it over here sooner, but I had to have a talk with your cousins."

"My cousins?" It's then I notice he's got a small cut on his lower lip. That's it, but I frown. "Did you guys... *fight?*"

"There wasn't much of a fight. A few punches thrown, but nothing major."

"If that's true, what happened to your lip?" I ask while reaching up to touch the spot I saw.

"Your cousin Black hits like a girl," he mumbles, moving in closer to me, one hand lazily resting against my back. His eyes hold me in place. I'm so caught up in them I can't breathe. All that beauty and I'm the focus of all of it. I couldn't look away if I tried.

"I think you might be the only man to ever say that," I tell him.

"Do friends kiss, Faith?"

"What?"

"I want to kiss you. Do friends kiss?"

"You do?"

"Definitely," he says bringing his face closer to mine. As he does, the contents of the bag he's holding gets closer and I catch the smell of bacon and eggs. I try to swallow it down, but I can't. I take off running because I can feel the bile rise in my stomach and I know what's coming. "Faith!" Titan calls from behind me, but I ignore him. I don't stop until I make it to the small guest bath in the hall. Then I dive toward the toilet.

I don't know if it's a minute later or maybe five, I just know I'm puking my guts out and Titan comes in and I want to die. There are several ways in life that you don't want a good looking man to find you. One of those high up on the list is puking. When I finish I feel a cool cloth hit my forehead and it's then I notice Titan is holding my hair out of the way and pressing a cloth to me. I take it and move it down to my lips, feeling horrible.

"Are you okay, Faith?" he asks, his voice quiet and gentle.

"Eggs," I manage to mutter.

"Eggs?"

"Zeus doesn't like eggs," I sigh.

"We're not naming our child Zeus," he says, but I can hear the smile behind his words—even if I can't see it.

"Can you give me a few minutes alone? I need to..."

"You're sure you're okay?"

"Yeah."

"Okay. Then I'll go get rid of the eggs."

"Much appreciated," I tell him, still not turning around to see him. *I'm too mortified.* He helps me stand, giving me a squeeze from behind, and then leaving the small room. Once the door closes I sink down to the commode and sit before my legs give out. This was not how I wanted Titan to see me. I rub my stomach absently, vowing again to never drink tequila again.

It takes some work, but I manage to make it back to my bedroom without Titan knowing. A few minutes later I emerge with my teeth brushed, and mouthwash taking away the stench from earlier. I've brushed my hair and put on clothes. I still feel nauseous, but at least I look human.

"How are you feeling?" he asks anxiously as I round the corner to the kitchen. He's sitting at the bar and it's clear he's worried.

"Fine. I just need some coffee."

"But—"

"It helps settle my stomach."

"Babe—"

Not wife... babe... it isn't bad, but it isn't wife. For some reason my brain fixates on that, but I push it down.

"It's decaf, Titan. Relax and while you're doing that, explain to me why you're here again."

"I wanted to surprise you before work. I was afraid I wouldn't make it. Aren't you going to be late?"

"Late? Oh... I don't work today, Titan. I uh... have an appointment."

"An appointment?" he asks and I finish fixing my coffee because I know what he's going to want and I'm not sure how I feel about it.

"I have a doctor's appointment today."

"About the baby?"

"Yeah..."

"I told you I wanted to go to those."

"Titan, it's my first real appointment since I moved here. It's not like they'll do a lot. You're more than welcome to come when they—"

"I'm coming to this one," he says obstinately and I sigh.

"What if I said no?"

"Then I'd follow you to the doctor appointment and stand outside the exam room," he says, his face devoid of any trace of emotion, but deathly serious in a way you could see, hear and *feel*.

"Fine. You can go, but I'm warning you right now, Big Daddy. You annoy me and I'll make them escort you out, and you won't be invited to any other appointments."

He shrugs and doesn't bother hiding his grin. I want to scream, but I stifle that and turn back to my coffee, urging it to hurry and finish. I've got a feeling I'm going to need its magical strength to get me through today.

41

TITAN

Ida Sue might be growing on me. When she suggested I take Faith breakfast this morning, I didn't readily agree. I didn't want to push my luck too soon. She kept insisting though—to the point of almost pushing me out the door. She knew about the doctor appointment. I thought the old woman was insane—and I still think that—but I'm starting to understand she's smart as a damn tack too. Crazy and smart is a combination any man should respect and be afraid of. Still, I definitely owe her one right now.

"How are you feeling, Ms. Lucas?" the doctor asks, making notes in his file.

"Good. A little tired, but not horrible," Faith answers, and I hear the nervousness in her voice.

"That's to be expected," the doctor says and he turns and grins at her. He's entirely too pretty. I don't like it. Doctors who deliver babies for a living are supposed to be old with kind faces, or... *women*. They aren't supposed to look pretty. They aren't supposed to be my age and if they are they don't need to be the doctor that looks at Faith. "Everything else seems to be okay? According to our records you're at your second month now, which is still rather early but you can notice a few changes."

"She got sick this morning," I answer for her when it becomes clear that Faith isn't going to bring it up. She huffs out a breath and gives me a mean look. I cross my arms at my chest and steadfastly ignore her.

"Sick?"

"The smell of eggs in the morning makes me sick. Titan didn't realize it and thought he was surprising me for breakfast," she explains with a sigh.

"Is this something new? Because of the baby?" the doctor prods.

"Yeah, it's just certain things: eggs, ground beef, and, ugh, anything with rosemary in it."

"Those are quite specific. This child might be a handful," the doctor laughs. I don't like his laugh either. It's entirely too personal. Like he's sharing some inside joke with my wife... *with Faith.*

"Just like her mother," I add with a smile and if my voice sounds territorial—it should.

The doctor glances at me and our eyes lock and he gets my message. I can see it on his face.

"Are you ready to hear the baby's heartbeat?" he asks, and damn if my own heart doesn't speed up. I've never been through this, didn't really know what to expect, but I didn't know I'd get to hear my child's heart... my child's heart... *beating.*

"More than ready," Faith says, smiling at the doctor, and I make a note that the first thing I'm going to insist on is finding a new doctor. An older one who has more experience... and a female one. *Definitely a female.*

I watch as he lifts Faith's shirt up. My gut tightens with dislike. I've never been possessive over a woman before in my life, but I'm definitely feeling that today with Faith. I won't bother denying it. I move in closer to Faith. She looks at me, her face shocked, and watches me even closer. I try not to flinch under her heavy gaze. Maybe she can see what's bothering me, though, because she grins.

"Easy, Big Daddy," she whispers and just like that, the worry is gone. I don't know how I managed to get my ass tied in knots over Faith, but I think it's clear I have. I just need to make sure she does the same. I reach over and take her hand in mine. Her smile falters, her gaze moves to our now joined hands and then slowly back to my face. I give her hand a gentle squeeze and her face goes sweet.

I haven't been paying attention. Not until the sound echoes in the room, but the doctor has an instrument of some kind on Faith's stomach and it's picking up the baby's heartbeat. It's fast... so fast my immediate reaction is something is wrong.

"What's wrong with him?" I ask before I can stop myself.

"Not a thing. It's a perfectly healthy heartbeat, one hundred and twenty beats per minute."

"One hundred and twenty? Is that normal?" Faith asks.

"I promise it's fine," the doctor says and he pats her hand. I don't stop the growl that bubbles out. Faith's face jerks to me and her eyes get round as saucers. She gives me a look that's meant to censure me, but I just shrug. If possible, her eyes get larger.

She needs to get used to it... and apparently, so do I.

FAITH

"I can't believe you growled at Dr. Brankins," I laugh as Titan pulls his car into my driveway.

"He was touching you," Titan mutters.

"He was trying to be reassuring!"

"He was being annoying."

"You're crazy," I say with a sigh. He turns off his car and then moves so he's looking right at me.

"You need a woman doctor."

"You can't be serious, Titan."

"I am serious and this guy was way too young. He can't have delivered very many babies at all. You need someone who knows what they're doing."

"Dr. Brankins delivered everyone of Kayla's, CC's and Petal's babies. They love him."

"Is that supposed to make me feel better? Because so far I'm thinking all of your cousins are insane and your aunt is a walking poster child for straightjackets."

"That's not nice, Titan," I tell him, but it takes work to keep from laughing. I mean, he's not completely wrong.

"The only thing that quack doctor made sense about was I

needed to watch over you more, and make note of things that bother you and watch for problems."

"Um... I don't remember him saying that, Big Daddy."

"He clearly said it," Titan argues.

I get out of the car, because I've got a really bad feeling about this. Titan has a look in his eye that scares me and maybe excites me—*which scares me more.*

"He did *not* say that, Titan."

"Babe, he did," he argues. He puts his hand at my back and walks us up my sidewalk toward the front door.

"When, Titan? When did he say that?"

"You were in the restroom. He said you needed someone to watch over you and make sure you got enough rest and ate right."

"I don't believe you," I argue and I have no idea why his words are making me panic, but they are.

"Can't help that, babe. It's true," he says and when I look up at him, he's grinning. I'm thinking that grin means bad things for me. "What's this?" he asks and I hadn't realized we were at the door already. He picks up a large white box. There's a giant red bow on it.

"I don't know," I answer. "Maybe Hope sent me something, or perhaps Charity got my letter about the baby and sent something."

"It has your name on it, but nothing else." He flicks the gift tag on top of the box.

"Bring it inside and I'll open it there. I know I'm not that far along but I swear I have to pee again."

"The romance has really left our relationship, hasn't it?" Titan jokes as I unlock the door.

"I don't think we have a relationship, remember? Divorced?"

"Annulled... and we're about to be parents together, so..."

"Please don't finish that sentence. I'm not sure I can handle much more today," I laugh, only half kidding.

He places the box on the table and I lift the top off and look down inside.

I pull out an old worn Dallas Cowboys football jersey. At first I don't realize what it is, and then it hits me. It's Brad's shirt. My ex-boyfriend, the creep who has been calling and the creep that hit me and knocked me on the ground because I had the nerve to tell him I didn't want to go to a party with him.

I used to sleep in this shirt every night—back when things were good. They hadn't been good for a long time. They were bad long before he hit me. Any feelings I had for him were long gone way before he hit me. The hit just gave me the courage to finally leave. I drop the jersey on the table.

"Dallas cowboys?" Titan asks, but I barely hear him.

It feels like blood is rushing through me and I can hear my heart beating in my ears. That's how much this reminder of my time with Brad bothers me. There are two other things in the box and I reach in and get those. One is a 5x7 picture in a silver frame. It's a picture of Brad and me one week after we met. It was our first official date. He flew me to Hawaii and had a private dinner served for us on a beach. He pulled out all of the stops. I thought I'd finally found something good in my life... someone who cared about me. We'd been dancing on the water's edge, barefoot, and I used my phone to take a selfie of us with the ocean and the sunset as our backdrop.

I used to love that picture.

"Faith?" Titan's voice again, but still I can't pay it attention.

I look at the folded piece of paper which was inside and open it up, barely noticing my hand is shaking.

Faith,

We were so good together. I miss you, Sunshine. Come home to me. You'll always be the only woman for me. We'll start over.

Brad.

I drop the note on the table and run to the bathroom, feeling the bile rise through me just like this morning. I'm going to be sick again and this time the cause is much worse than just the smell of eggs.

43

TITAN

I should run after Faith, but something upset her and right now, with anger—and jealousy—firing through me, I don't. I pick up the note she dropped and read it. I read it again and then I wad the bastard up in my hand. Then I take in the picture of a smiling Faith with a man I don't know, but a man who was holding her close and doing it while smiling—not at the camera, but at her, and I don't like that at all. Then I look at the faded jersey—obviously a man's and obviously well worn. I like that and the fact a man sent it to her even less.

I throw it all back in the box, because I don't want to see it. I actually have to fight the urge to take it out and burn it. I do that barely, though I make a note to do it later if Faith doesn't have an issue with it.

But that's the thing that's bothering me the most.

Is she upset because she has feelings for this... *Brad*? Or is she upset for a different reason? I finally control enough of my reaction—and I know most of it is unreasonable—to follow her into the master bathroom.

I saw pictures of this place and floor plans before I agreed to my contract. So I know the layout. That said, walking into the master bedroom, it's all different. In here, Faith has definitely put her stamp on the place. She's painted the walls a calming gray which you would think would be washed out with her white furniture, but it's not. It feels peaceful. Of course the yellow curtains and throw pillows on the bed covered in white, along with plush yellow rugs on the floor scream vibrant and happy, like Faith herself—or like the Faith I remember in Vegas...

I walk into the bathroom and Faith is at the sink now, splashing water on her face. There's a small cup and an open bottle of mouthwash there too. Clearly I took way too long looking at the shit *Brad* sent. I should have been in here, seeing to her.

"You okay, Faith?"

Her eyes come to mine in the mirror and I see the circles under them that makeup hid before. She's not been sleeping. That much is clear. *Another gut punch.* I feel like I'm missing a huge piece to the puzzle, but one thing is crystal clear. Faith has not been taking care of herself. She needs someone to watch over her and clearly, I've been dragging my feet when I should have just taken control from the beginning. There's a time to take things slow and I thought that was how to deal with Faith.

I was wrong. I thought I was wrong after the doctor visit and now I *know* I was.

"Titan... I—"

"Who's Brad?" I ask before she can finish.

That troubled look moves through her face again and I can feel the tension from her body tighten.

"A mistake," she says softly, almost so softly I can't hear.

"Come here, Faith," I order her, but I do it gently. She needs gentle from me right now and because of that I tap down any of the jealousy and anger I didn't get a handle on before. Surprisingly, she walks to me. I take her into my arms and she buries her face into my chest. I feel a shudder go through her and I hold her tighter, letting my fingers drift through her hair. "Talk to me," I tell her quietly.

Her body pushes deeper into mine, her nails bite into my back and again her body trembles. Without thought, I pick her up and carry her into the bedroom. I sit on the bed and lean back against the headboard, bringing her against my chest and holding her.

She looks up at me with tears in her eyes. She hasn't shed them, but the moisture is gathered—I can see them, and I do not like them. Whatever she's about to tell me, I already know that I'm not going to like this Brad.

Not at all.

44

FAITH

I don't know how long I've been in Titan's arms. I don't know and I don't care. It feels like heaven and it's something I've wanted since I left him in Colorado. As stupid as it sounds, it feels like coming home. He doesn't question me further, he just holds me, his fingers sifting through my hair and his heartbeat vibrating in my ear. I want to stay like this, but I know I need to explain why I got upset. I need to tell him about Brad, if only because Brad seems to be intent on making sure I don't forget him. So I take a deep, shuddering breath and pull my head from Titan's chest to look up at him.

"Brad was my boyfriend," I tell him and Titan's face goes tight. I don't know how I know what he's thinking, but I do, and I reach up to move my thumb along the side of his chin. "I left him months before I ever met you in Vegas. He's part of the reason I knew relationships and marriage weren't ever going to be a part of my plan."

"That ugly?" he asks, his voice so quiet that I don't believe I've ever heard him talk that soft. "You seemed happy in that picture," he adds and I know he didn't mean it to sound like an accusation, but that's how it feels. I'm just sensitive right now.

As always, when dealing with anything related to Brad, I feel stupid.

"That picture wasn't long after I met him and it was our first real date. I had stars in my eyes. Brad was the first man who ever acted like he cared about me. Hell, except for my dad, sisters, and my dad's family, he was the only person. Which I guess, thinking on it, made me an easy mark."

"How long were you with him?"

"Two years."

"That's a long time," Titan says and he's not wrong, but he's also not right.

"I would have left him—*should* have left him way before I did. It hadn't been good for over a year."

"Why didn't you leave?"

"I'm not sure. At first I thought it would get better, just a rough patch and all couples go through it... You know?" I ask, looking up at him. He nods slightly, but doesn't speak, so I keep going. "But then, the arguments got louder, darker, and every time I started to leave Brad would do something to show me he loved me and was willing to start over. It began this cycle I never seemed to break free of. We'd fight, he'd break stuff and scare me, but he always apologized and promised to do better. He had a way of twisting words that made me feel like the fight... like our problems were all my fault. That I didn't work hard enough to understand him, that I was the one failing him."

Titan growls under his breath and holds me tighter. I curl deeper into him, soaking in the warmth of his body and letting it comfort me.

"Finish it, babe," he says and again—I mourn the loss of the way he used to say wife.

Maybe I really am losing my mind.

"One night he came home. It was like three in the morning, and sadly, that was nothing new. He was drunk and again that wasn't much different than the normal either."

"Fucking loser," Titan says and he's not that wrong.

"Yeah," I whispered.

"Had a good woman at home, ignored that. Took advantage of that and pissed it away. Fucking loser," he says expanding his thoughts in a way that makes me feel a warm shiver run through my body and this one is all good. I lean up and kiss the corner of his chin, lightly in appreciation. I would have rather had his lips, but I couldn't quite reach that far unless Titan bent down. He didn't so I got what I could. That said, I had the taste of his skin on my tongue and that wasn't a bad thing at all. "Finish it and then we'll forget him," Titan says, giving my body a squeeze.

"This time he had lipstick on his collar and he reeked of perfume—not my brand, not even close. When I asked him about it, he told me not to worry about it, that he brought his dick home to me." Titan's arms get tighter with that announcement, but I push through. "When he began undressing he told me to do the same. I didn't want to be with him. Lately I hardly ever wanted to. I'd have to force myself sometimes. But that night, with him drunk and smelling like another woman—I really didn't want to. He grabbed me and pinned me on the bed, and I fought him."

"Motherfucker, I'll kill him," Titan growls, and the anger coming off of him now is huge. So huge it takes over the air in the room.

"Titan—"

"Finish it, Faith," he orders and I swallow down my nerves.

"He ripped my panties and was about to rape me."

"Finish it," he growls when I stop, his voice so dark that I feel like I need to comfort him. I try to do that by holding him closer and kissing his neck. He shudders, and then says again, "Finish it." This time his voice is softer, so maybe I helped some.

"I panicked. I know... I mean, with us and what we've done, Titan... You may not believe me, but I never, *never* have sex without protection. I insist on it. Life with my mother taught me that. I was scared of him raping me, but I would have endured it... But the thought of him taking that from me and not wearing a condom... it's stupid. I know it's stupid because it all was bad, but I couldn't let him put my body at risk. I had to fight harder. So I did. I bit him. I did it hard enough that my mouth filled with blood and I didn't let go until he let go of my wrists and hit me."

"Son of a bitch!"

"Then, when I got free from his hold, I pushed my thumbs into his eyes hard like they teach you in those self-defense classes. He fell back and he swung at me again. He hit me hard enough that I was dizzy, but I managed to shake that off. I had so much adrenaline running through me. I managed to knee him in the balls. He fell from the bed and he was on the floor. The rest is kind of a haze. I remember running to the master bathroom. I locked the door and stayed there. He never came after me. I was so scared. I thought he would, but he didn't. I started cleaning out my closet—it was in there and I got dressed and threw everything I could in my suitcase. I can remember choking on fear when I opened the door, but when I walked into the bedroom he was passed out on the floor snoring. I left and I didn't look back."

"You didn't press charges?"

"I didn't. I thought about it, but Brad had friends in the police department and judges he rubbed elbows with. I didn't see doing that helping me. I just wanted away from him."

"And he let you go?"

"He'd call here and there and ask me to come back. I took a couple of the calls, but I told him it was over. When he kept calling, I changed my number and made plans to leave Vegas."

"And the night we met?"

"I'd run into Brad for the first time that morning. He was at the casino. He heard my sister was getting married. Black was with me and he intimidated Brad so he left. But I knew... if I didn't leave Vegas that Brad would never let me see peace."

"You should have told me this sooner," Titan says, his voice rumbling.

"Why?"

"Are you shitting me?"

"Titan, we weren't in a relationship, and you followed me to make that official. There's no reason I would have told you."

"Fair enough. Then here's a warning you need to take to heart, Faith."

"A warn—"

"We're in a relationship from this moment on. You're carrying my baby. *Mine*. We're in a relationship and you're *mine*. That gives it to you officially and I do not let anyone fuck with what is mine. You get it?"

"I... *We're in a relationship*?"

"That's what I said."

"Do I get a say here?"

"You do," he confirms so I breathe a little easier.

"Then I don't think—"

"You get to agree we're in a relationship and that you understand no one is going to fuck with you from this moment on."

I take a breath. I look at Titan and his face is stoic, heated, intense and it's not all bad. In fact, I like a lot of what he's saying. I've also missed him. Missed him so much I wake up aching. Still...

"Can you define relationship?" I ask, thinking we can start slowly and begin dating. We skipped that whole part, and dating Titan might be fun.

"I'll define it for you," he says and I breathe easier.

"That'd be good," I smile, hoping to ease his mood, because he's still really intense.

"I'm moving in," he announces and I jump in his arms. I look at his face, which is set in stone.

Oh crap.

45

TITAN

"Thanks for bringing my shit over," I tell Black, who is standing at the door. He hands me my suitcase, but he hasn't spoken and he refuses to move. I wait and there's still no response. "Are you going to talk?"

"Faith is okay with you moving in here?"

"What the hell is that supposed to mean?"

"Exactly what it means."

"If she wasn't, do you think I'd be standing here?"

"I don't really know you, Titan. Except that you were an asshole to my cousin when she needed you to be a man. So to answer your question, I don't know."

I drop my bags on the floor and cross my arms, daring him to talk more shit. He's not wrong; I was a dick to Faith when she told me about the baby. But until Black has chased a woman and had her walk out on him twice and then get sucker punched like I did that day at the church, he can shut his fucking mouth.

After Faith's story about her ex, I'm needing a few things to punch and Black's face is as good as any. We stand there, neither of us giving an inch, until Faith comes in from the kitchen.

"What's going on?" she asks, immediately picking up on the tension in the room.

"I was just explaining to Titan that I wasn't sure you really wanted him staying here," Black says, his eyes not leaving mine.

"I was just explaining to Black he could go fuck himself," I respond, not blinking.

"So really you guys are in a pissing match."

Both of us grunt in reply to her.

"Black, I got to warn you, if the two of you are going to get in a contest to see who has the biggest dick, Titan will win."

"What?" we both ask again, our gazes jerking to her instantly. Faith is leaning against the side of the sofa staring at both of us.

"I'm just saying that I've seen both and Titan's is bigger. So if we could wrap this up sometime today, that'd be swell."

"I doubt it's bigger," Black grumbles under his breath.

"When did you see his dick?"

I turn to face Faith then and before I had just been thinking about punching Black in the face. *Now I need to.*

"Several times."

"*Several times*?" I bark.

"You've never seen it hard and ready though, and damn it, it's plenty big. Probably bigger than this asshole's," Black mutters from behind me. He must have decided to come inside because he slams the door.

"I love you, Black, but it's not."

"*When* did you see his dick?" I growl again.

"Titan?"

"Answer me, Faith."

"Oh my God! Are you jealous?"

"I want to know when you saw Black's dick."

"Several times," she grins and it's a grin that has her daring me to spank her ass.

"Tell me when," I growl.

"I'll have you know some women are afraid of my dick when

they see it because it's so big," Black grumbles and God, I really want to punch him.

"Well, the first time I think I was three," she grins and Christ, she's busting my balls and enjoying it.

"It was even big back then."

"Will you shut up about the size of your dick," I growl.

"I just want it on record that my dick is not small. I've never had a complaint either, not one, and there's been plenty of women, let me tell you. *Plen—tee*!"

I roll my eyes at him and pinch the bridge of my nose.

"So you've only seen his dick when you were kids. Quit trying to make me hit him, Faith."

"I saw it again when I was four, maybe five," she says smiling sweetly.

"You were older. What were you doing showing a kid your damn dick?" I growl, mad all over again and ready to kill Black.

"I'm not that much older! And we were playing farm. Plus, again, I'd like to point out that we were kids and my dick is definitely bigger now. Plus, *again*, I was not hard. There was no erection. It's unfair to judge a man when he's not rose to the occasion."

"What the fuck is farm? You white people are fucking nuts," I growl and Faith bursts out laughing.

It's a beautiful sound, and she's damn gorgeous—so gorgeous it hurts to look at her. So gorgeous that looking at her like this helps rid me of some of my anger. After what she shared with me earlier today and the pain I saw on her face, her laugh almost makes this shit worth it. I haven't seen her this happy—this close to being the Faith I was drawn to, since we were in Buck-Stop and she was telling those old men I was a chick. Twisted as it is, I like it enough my bad mood is almost completely gone.

"Farm. Black, Blue, Hope, and I used to play it."

"Blue?"

"Black's twin. I don't think you've met him. He's been out of town."

"Jesus, there's two of you?"

"I'm the best, and might I add, I have the biggest dick of the two of us."

"Your brother is named Blue," I mumble, thinking it's official that Ida Sue is the craziest woman I've ever met in my life. "What is farm and why in the hell couldn't they play it with Petal or Maggie?"

"That's our sister, C.T. What you're suggesting is sick."

"What?"

"It's farm, where you milk the cows and throw corn out to the chickens, that kind of thing."

"Milk the cow... You touched her breasts?"

"Well, technically they were udders," Black says.

"You fucking pervert, and you let her touch your dick?"

"Well, that wasn't part of the game." Black shrugs.

"Then why did she touch it?" I turn to look at Faith. "Why did *you* touch it?"

"I'd never seen one and if they were going to touch my boobs, I was going to touch whatever they had."

"I... Where in the hell were your parents while all this was going on?"

"You probably don't want to ask that right now," Black says.

"Is this only time you saw Black's dick?"

"Well, no. I was staying the night with Petal and Black was out in the barn with that girl. What was her name? Do you remember, Black?"

"Not really. There's been a lot of girls. Because *I have a very big dick*."

"Oh, come on, you can't forget her," Faith argues.

I'm starting to get a headache.

"A very big dick which is *highly* in demand," he adds. Jesus.

"Remember, Black," Faith continues, ignoring him. "She was dating White at the time."

"Ohhh... You mean Candy."

"Yeah! God, she was such an airhead. She was an insult to

blondes. Really, women like her is why blondes have bad names," Faith huffs. "I wonder whatever happened to her?"

"She was a porn star for a while. At least until her fake boobs burst."

"Oh my God! They burst?" Faith cries.

"Yeah. Don't worry, though. Her husband does that shit for a living. She's like a Double V now."

"Double V?" I ask, because I can't keep up with her crazy, but fuck, Double V tits are worth at least looking at once in your life.

"Yeah, and I know what you're thinking, C.T."

"Doubtful."

"I do, but you're wrong. Some things should not be seen. You never get it out of your head. Turns out boobs *can* be too big—unlike dicks. Did I mention my dick is above average in size? And width really. Everyone knows that width is more important too."

"You need to let it go, Black," I start, but I don't get the rest of my thought out because a throw pillow hits me in the head.

"C.T.?"

"Faith—"

"As in the C.T. that owns this fucking house?"

"Faith—"

"As in the C.T. with a temperature so huge he couldn't be bothered to come and collect the rent? *That C.T.?*"

"Fuck, sorry, man. It just slipped out," Black says, but I ignore him. I'm concentrating on Faith.

A very pissed off Faith.

46

FAITH

"That is not cool of you, Ida Sue. We're family and you always told me family can depend on each other."

"And we can, even when one is being stubborn as a mule and needs a lot of help getting out of the barn shed."

"You knew I wanted to stand on my own. I didn't want Titan's help. I got myself into this situation and..."

"I'm thinking his ding dong helped get you that way."

"His ding dong?"

"Not all my nicknames can be golden, dear. I get it. You're mad I let C.T. stand up and be a man, which he should have been from the beginning. I'd feel guilty but there's people starving in the world. There's bigger problems than you having a god put a bun in your oven and wanting to play house. Are we done here?"

"You're so annoying, Ida Sue."

"Runs in the family, Blossom. Now, if you don't mind I need to go. My man has decided to remind me who I belong to and he's in a pretty festive mood since my resident eye candy just moved out of the house."

"Fine, go. But this isn't the last you're going to hear about it."

"Didn't suspect it would be. You are a Lucas after all. Tell C.T. bye for me."

"What does C.T. stand for anyways?"

"Chocolate Thunder," she giggles and hangs up.

I stare at my cellphone for a minute and turn it off, shaking my head.

"What does C.T. stand for?" Titan asks.

He's sitting on my bed, which I guess is his bed. After I yelled at him, I called Ida Sue. Black left somewhere in the middle of the argument and I yelled at him before that. Which means I've yelled a lot this evening, and it changed nothing.

"Chocolate Thunder," I mumble, too tired to lie to him.

"Christ. Your aunt is fucking looney."

"Titan, we have to talk."

"Faith, I'm not fighting with you about this anymore. It's stupid."

"It's not stupid. You bought a house—"

"I'm coaching a D-league team. It was part of the deal. I get to still take part in the sport I love and I can do it being close to my woman and my child. I lost nothing in this deal."

"But..."

"There are no buts," he says and I want to choke him.

"There are! If this was the deal you wanted, then why even go through the whole wedding with Jacey!"

"Damn it, Faith!"

"Unless you have feelings for her. Oh my God, is that what this is all about? Do you have feelings for her? I destroyed everything with my announcement, didn't I?"

Titan growls—literally growls—and stomps over to me.

"Stop it. I swear to God I can't handle much more today. I had a plan and it was a good plan, because I didn't have anything else in my life. Nothing good. It was just life. Then one night with a crazy-ass blonde turned my world upside down."

"Titan—"

"A crazy-ass blonde who haunts my dreams so much that I can't get her out of my mind."

"Titan—"

"A crazy-ass blonde whose taste stays on my tongue, whose touch is burned into my skin and whose voice stays in my head."

"Titan—"

"That happened before I knew about our baby, Faith."

"Titan—"

"It happened before you were in the church that day."

"Damn it, Titan—" I try again, my voice shaking, emotion surging through me.

"It's just one of the reasons I was already calling the wedding off. It's you I want, Faith. I don't care how we started. I just know this is how I want it to go. I want to be with you. I want to build something with you, with our child and—"

"Jesus, Titan—" I whisper and tears are clogging my throat.

"I don't care how we started, Faith," he says again and he's standing right in front of me. His amber colored eyes are shining down at me so bright they sparkle, even through my tears. "I don't care about any of it. But I'm here because in the end, it's you I want with me."

"Are you finished?" I ask.

His hand comes up to slide against my neck, his thumb moving back and forth gently on my chin.

"For now," he says, his lips moving into a soft smile.

"Then can you shut up and kiss me?" I ask him.

In answer, he pulls my face to him and his lips press against mine in the sweetest whisper-soft touch I've ever felt... *and it's never been better.*

47

TITAN

I pick Faith up and carry her to the bed. I didn't plan for things to go this way, but I'm not stopping. Since Faith left me in Colorado, I've barely been getting through the day. I wasn't lying. She's been haunting me and having her stand there and dare to think I'd want anyone over her is more than I can handle.

When I made the move to Texas, I didn't expect this. I wanted to make sure Faith and the baby were taken care of. I wanted to be a part of my child's life. What I didn't expect was to be drawn even deeper to Faith. I should have. God knows she's a fever in my blood—but yet, I didn't.

I stand her up by the edge of the headboard. The only sound in the room is our breathing, both ragged. The feel of the room is electric. It's been too long since we were together, and this is different. Before we had no direction; we came together out of need and pleasure. Now... *Fuck*. Hopefully now we're going somewhere. We're together, because I'm not letting her go.

I undress her slowly. Her eyes hold mine the whole time and she doesn't stop me. If anything she helps, and when she's completely naked she does something to surprise me further. She doesn't hide her body. Instead she reaches over and pulls on my shirt. I help slide it over my head, throwing it down on the floor with hers. Once that's done she moves her hand over my chest. Her touch is like a drug. I missed it, but until this moment I didn't realize how much. Her fingers slide over my ribs, under my pecs and up to my neck. They press in there, taking in my pulse and holding me. Her gaze locks with mine and then she gives it to me. She gives it to me so sweetly that I didn't know it was the one thing I missed the most, until I have it.

"I've missed you, Big Daddy."

There it was. There it fucking was.

She missed me. Even with her whacked nickname I soak in that beauty coming from her. I've never had that in my life either. Had people come and go. Some people meant a lot, others just pass through. But not one ever looked at me and said they missed me—not with meaning, not with emotion thick in their voice, so thick you knew they truly meant it. *Not until Faith.*

Her hands go to my belt and she slowly undoes it. Her hand trembles and somehow that tremble moves through me. I cup her hand in mine, holding it still. Again her eyes come back to mine.

"I've missed you, *wife*."

I don't know what makes me say the words, I just know they feel right. I see exactly when they hit Faith. Her face reflects shock, but then she smiles and it's a smile that lights the room.

"Let's get you naked," she whispers and on that we can completely agree. I undo the button while she's already sliding the zipper down. I shove my clothes down and step out of them. I'd like to say I played it slow and cool, but fuck, I just want them out of the way. Hell, when I kick my shoe off it goes sailing through the air and hits a lamp. Faith jumps into my body as it crashes into the floor in a heap of broken glass.

"I'll buy you a new one," I grumble and she looks up at me with her mouth open and then she laughs, so happy and free something squeezes in my heart.

"Anxious?" she asks, when she finally gains control again.

"Like you wouldn't believe," I admit without blinking.

"I'm not going anywhere," she whispers.

"So, you're saying I'm going to wake up and you'll be here with me for a change?"

"That's the plan," she agrees.

"So, no handcuffs are needed?"

"Not this round, but maybe next time..." She grins seductively, leaving little doubt at what she's talking about.

"Making note," I tell her as I gather her in my arms and bring her down on the bed with me.

I lay her on her back, as I go to my side so I can look at her. I hold one of her breasts, letting the weight of it settle in my hand.

Perfection.

"I love your body. Light to my dark, smooth to my rough, soft to my hard," I rumble in her ear, biting on the lobe. I suck it into my mouth while squeezing her nipple and then kneading her breast.

"Definitely hard," she whispers, her hand wrapping around my cock and squeezing. I close my eyes as pleasure ripples through my body. I thrust into her hand before I can stop myself.

"Keep that up and this party will end way too soon," I warn her, kissing down her neck and shoulder.

"That would be a shame, but I do love touching you, Titan," she says, squeezing my cock again.

I run my tongue along the indention of her collarbone, nibbling gently on the skin. Then I move lower, taking her nipple into my mouth, sucking it while I squeeze her breast, and then I move my hand to play with her other nipple, while still sucking the first. I tease them at the same time, playing them against each other. Tugging, biting, licking, sucking, all done to drive her wild. Her fingers stab into my shoulder as her body rhythmically rocks. Her moan triggers my growl as I abandon her breasts and move farther down.

My hand rests on her stomach. And I spread it out, palm down and just hold it there. She brings her hand down, placing it over mine.

"Our baby," I whisper, emotion thick in my voice.

"You want him."

"Or her," I groan, moving down to kiss the top of her hand.

"I was scared you would be mad..."

"I'm the one who didn't protect you, Faith," I tell her, taking full responsibility.

"Most men don't want a baby taking over their life and ruining—"

"Our baby is giving me everything I want and more, even if I didn't realize it. Our child is a blessing, not a mistake," I add, needing her to know exactly how I feel.

Then, I move my hand down lower.

48

FAITH

I feel Titan's hand move between my legs and my breath catches in my throat. I've missed him. My eyes close as his fingers drift against my clit. My body convulses with the first swipe—the joy is that intense.

"You're already primed, aren't you, Faith? I could make you come so easily, just from brushing against your clit," he whispers against my thigh. I don't answer him. I'm too busy drinking in all of the sensations that are sweeping through me. His heated touch, warm breath, the weight of his body leaning on me, it feels so good, all of it... all of *him*.

"Titan," I moan when I feel one of his fingers—or maybe two —push inside of me.

"Spread your legs wider for me, Faith," he urges before biting into my thigh. I cry at the sting of pain, and my body surges up and causes his fingers to sink a little deeper. "Spread them," Titan growls, his voice hoarse and intense.

As I come back down, I instantly plant the heels of my feet against the bed and spread my legs. I thought he'd get between them, but he doesn't. Instead, he bends over my thigh and brings his tongue straight to my clit, his fingers still buried inside of me.

He flicks his tongue over my clit while his fingers push in and then withdraw inside of me. With each thrust his fingers press against the walls of my pussy, almost scraping them in a move that feels so good I can do nothing but cry out.

"That's it baby. That's it," Titan praises against my pussy and then he's sucking on my clit, manipulating it—*worshipping it*—with his mouth. My hands tangle into the sheet I'm lying on as I try to hold back. Titan doesn't allow that, though, because he moves his mouth and then his hand comes down and spanks my throbbing clit at the exact moment his fingers tunnel deep inside.

"Titan!" I cry, as wave after wave of need crashes over me. I'm so close to my orgasm that I can practically taste it. "Please, baby. I need you in me when I come," I tell him, my head going back and forth as it builds. When I come, I know it's going to be more intense than anything I've felt before.

I thought he would move and take me while I was under him, but Titan surprises me again. He turns me to my side, two of his fingers still inside of me—though not moving.

"Hook your leg over mine," he growls in my ear.

I'm so far gone that at first I'm not sure what he means. Still, I hook my foot behind his calf. Titan's hand wraps around my knee and he pulls my leg up higher.

I moan with frustration and sadness when his fingers leave my pussy, but I don't have time to protest, because a minute later I feel the head of his cock pushing at my entrance from behind me. That's good. *That's unbelievably good.* Anticipation spreads through me as he pulls me back against him even deeper. His large arm locks around my upper torso, his hand grabbing my breast and squeezing it rhythmically just as his cock pushes in deeper.

He doesn't hurry when he does this. He goes slow and I take him inside in a lazy slow stroke that leaves me swearing I can feel every inch as it breaches me. Feel, memorize and let it brand me. My head goes back against his shoulder. His heavy breath is right there and I hear him groan as he plants himself so deep I can feel his balls pushing against me.

He's never been this deep in me before. I've never felt this stretched, this full... *and it feels perfect—better than perfect.*

"You're mine, Faith," he whispers.

"Titan," I cry as he begins to withdraw. I grind my ass against him, doing my best to keep him with me—inside of me.

He doesn't speed up; he keeps the ride slow and steady, but he doesn't stop working my breast, he doesn't stop holding me and whispering soft words of praise in my ear. It's delicious and beautiful. So beautiful that I don't even try to stop it when my orgasm hits.

"That's it, Faith. Come all over my cock, woman. Come all over it," he growls before biting into my shoulder, and that too feels good.

"I've missed you, Titan. God, baby. I've missed you."

I just keep saying that over and over while I ride out my release. I can't think, I just need him to know that. A moment later I feel his body tighten. A moment after that he's filling me with his cum. Jet after jet unleashes almost as powerful as his thrusts, and in that moment I don't think it can get any better. I seriously don't, but then Titan proves me wrong when he whispers in my ear.

"Feels like coming home, Faith. Fuck me, you feel like coming home."

49

TITAN

"If I'm dreaming, don't wake me," I mumble, still planted deep inside of Faith. Our breathing is normal again and I have her held against me. She has one hand reaching back to hold my hip and another tangled with the one I have over her breasts. I lean up so I can see her face and she's smiling. Her eyes are closed and that sweet smile is wide. My woman is happy. Fuck, so am I. I know I missed her. I didn't realize how much until I got inside of her.

"I think that's my line, Big Daddy," she laughs. I bury my head into her neck, fake growling while nibbling on her, and she giggles louder.

She moves as I tickle her and I growl for real when she moves on my cock. I should be spent, but I'm still hard. My dick shudders from deep inside of her, wanting to move more. Faith has to feel it too because she grinds her ass against me with a moan of pleasure.

"Hungry for more?" I ask, my fingers curling into her thigh.

"I shouldn't be, but you feel so good."

"Now that's my line," I joke. I move my hand from her hip, and capture hers. I bring it up and stare at it. Her pale skin shines against mine. Her long slender fingers look graceful. Her hands are just as beautiful as the rest of her. I kiss her fingers, my thumb brushing over one in particular.

"What did you do with your wedding ring?" I ask her before I can stop myself.

Her body tenses slightly.

"I guess I should have given it back to you."

"Why? It's yours. I gave it to you," I answer, kissing the finger where the ring was.

"You could have gotten your money back for something. You could have probably used it for Ja—"

"Don't say it. Don't ruin what just happened, and don't ruin how fucking amazing it feels to still be inside of you by bringing up how stupid I was."

"Oh... I didn't mean anything bad," she whispers, and she turns her head to look up at me. "I promise. We didn't owe each other anything at that point."

"Does that mean you think we do now?"

"Well... I think now, if you left me to go marry another woman I'd be a little upset."

I grin.

"A little?"

"Okay, more than a little," she mumbles and she blushes as she admits it. "I'd probably sic Black on you... or maybe Leroy."

"Good to know, but I'm not planning on going out and marrying another woman, so I think I'm safe. So, where's your ring?"

"In the nightstand drawer, why?"

"Just wondering," I lie. I want it back on her finger. But I'll hold off on that. I don't want to change her mood while my dick is deep inside of her and her hips are moving slowly as she starts to ride me. She's doing it in a way that I don't think she realizes it—at least not fully, and that makes it sweeter.

"Where's yours?" she says, her voice husky and threaded with need.

"In my suitcase," I tell her, not adding that I look at it every night. Now's not the time for that either. I move my hand up her stomach and then farther up to her breasts.

"Titan..."

"I think you're hungry, Faith. Am I right?"

"Yes..." she whimpers as I tweak her nipple.

I'm about to shift our position when the phone rings.

"Expecting someone?"

"No. It's probably Ida Sue or Black. They call almost every night."

"Don't move," I grumble. She moves on my cock again in response.

"Can't promise that, Big Daddy."

"I'm going to spank your ass," I growl, stretching to get the phone, while still remaining inside Faith.

I bring the phone up and frown because it says, *"Unknown Caller."*

I click it on, bringing it to my ear. Before I can say hello a man is talking.

"Hey, Sunshine, hope I didn't wake you. I just wanted to see if you got my present."

Brad.

My body tenses and I know Faith feels it because she turns and it causes my cock to slide out of her.

Yet another reason to hate this Brad.

"Titan?" she asks worriedly.

"She got them, but got to tell you, Brad. I'm not real big on you sending presents to my wife."

"Who is this?" he asks, his voice controlled and clipped.

"Faith's husband."

"She's married?"

"Very, and I'm a man who is not stupid."

"What does that mean?"

"It means I'm not an idiot who pisses away the best thing in his life. I'm also not a boy trying to be a man and use his fists on something precious. I think you get where I'm going with this," I tell him.

"Titan," Faith says softly, her arm hugging me close as she moves to look at me. I turn to watch her. Her face is anxious, but she's not upset with me.

"Let me speak to Faith," Brad orders.

"Sorry, *Brad*. She's busy right now."

"Busy? I want to speak to her."

"Yeah, busy. As in she's spread for me and about to take my cock. So you aren't speaking to her and while we're at it, don't call here anymore. Lose this number."

"I—"

I don't let the asshole finish. I hang up the phone.

Faith slides over top of my body and looks down at me, but she does this smiling and throwing the phone on the floor.

"You think that was necessary?" she asks, her voice betraying her need to laugh.

"It felt pretty damn good," I tell her.

"I bet I know something that will feel better," she says.

"What's that?" I ask, but my question ends with a moan as she wraps her hand around my cock and then shifts so she can slide down on him. She sits up on my lap, my cock filling her and she smiles down at me, like a fucking queen. Her hands brace on my stomach and she begins to ride me.

"Fuck yeah, Faith. Ride me," I growl and she does, taking us both to heaven and leaving *Brad* where he belongs...

In the past.

50

FAITH

"How are you doing?" Hope's voice comes over my phone as I pull into the drive.

"I'm getting fat," I laugh, rubbing my stomach.

"I doubt that seriously. You're not that far along," Hope answers.

"Yeah, but Titan has been cooking dinner every night for two weeks."

"Titan cooks?" she asks, surprised, and I look down at my lap, grinning wide.

"My man cooks," I whisper.

"You're really happy," Hope croons, her voice practically gleeful.

"I really am," I agree.

Hope squeals, proving her joy for me and there it is. As much as I dreaded my sisters telling me I was nothing but a screw up again, Hope proves she wants me to be happy. She loves me and I know Charity would be the same.

"Are you going back to Vegas?"

"What for?"

"All night chapels?"

"Um... no. Not again. I think one Elvis wedding in my life is one too many, sister dear."

"It doesn't have to be Elvis! How about Liberace? Or Gene Simmons?"

"Um... no, no and hell no," I laugh, thinking maybe I'm not the only one of my sisters who inherited some of Aunt Ida Sue's crazy genes.

"What about the Blues Brothers? Oh my God, Faithy! That could be so fun! You could both wear matching suits with the hats and the shades and—"

"And gee, Hope, the answer is no again."

"Okay, one last suggestion..."

"I can barely wait," I laugh.

"Two words. Jack Sparrow."

"What?"

"Girl! They have a pirate wedding package now! You can literally get married by Jack Sparrow."

"Hope—"

"And instead of saying I do you can say savvy instead!"

"Hope, seriously—"

"Faithy, you have to admit, Titan would look hot as hell dressed up like a pirate," she answers and that makes me stop for a minute as I imagine my man all dressed up in pirate gear. I have to admit that could be very hot.

"Hope, honey, I got to go."

"But we need to discuss this wedding. We could be slutty pirates! I have this costume that Aden would love... and you could get one to match. Titan won't know what hits him!"

"Hope, I don't even know if Titan wants to get married again. We haven't really talked about it."

And we haven't. If there's one black spot on the perfection that has been the last two weeks, it's that I don't really know where this relationship is going. I mean, I'm not asking for promises of forever, but maybe a sign that he's not just hanging around for the baby... and the hot sex.

Definitely the hot sex.

"Then maybe you ought to talk about it," she nudges.

"It's not that easy, Hope."

"It is. You're just being a wimp."

"What if he says he doesn't want to get married?"

"Then you live in sin like Aunt Ida Sue. She seems happy enough."

"I could, right? By the way, I'm totally ignoring that you actually said the phrase *'living in sin'*."

"You totally could. You love him. Right, little sis?"

"So much it hurts." I whisper the truth, and even saying it out loud makes my stomach flutter with nerves.

"Have you tried telling him that?"

"Well...no."

"And why not?"

"Because—"

"You do realize we have Lucas blood running through our veins."

"What does that mean?"

"It means we grab what we want by the horns. We don't let fear hold us back. Do you think it was easy for me to face Aden after everything I did?"

"No, I know it wasn't."

"It really wasn't, but look how that worked out."

"But Aden loves you," I argue.

"I didn't know that at the time, now did I? But there's something you're forgetting," she says calmly, like she has no idea of the terror swimming in the pit of my stomach right now.

"What's that?"

"Titan has chased after you since day one. A man doesn't do that unless he cares."

"He wanted an annulment."

"Bullshit. If that was it he could have had you served with papers. You weren't trying to hide. You still used your damn credit cards and you called me almost every day."

I take a deep breath and think over her words. I feel hope begin to bubble up inside of me. Titan did tell me he wanted me. He didn't use the word love, but what he did say was more than I ever hoped to have. It was really good. And if the last two weeks are a sample of what life with Titan would be like, then I definitely want that.

"I'll talk to him tonight," I agree, closing my eyes and praying I'm not making a mistake.

"Good girl. I'm proud of you. Call me and let me know when I need to get my pirate getup dry cleaned."

"You're a freak, Hope."

"Takes one to know one, sister dear."

"Love you, freak."

"Love you, too."

I hang up the phone and stare at the house. Then I grab my stuff, open the door and take a breath. Praying I'm doing the right thing.

51

TITAN

I look around the room, wondering if I have everything right. I'm actually freaking nervous, which I've never been before. Then again, nothing has ever been this important to me—not even winning the championship. I look down at my championship ring and frown. Before Faith came into my life, football was all I had. That was it. Now it's not even important. I went to work coaching the D-league players on a team that pretty much stinks. There's a challenge there and we have some promising guys. I can build it and it makes me happy and I think in the end a few of these guys may get sent up to the pros. I enjoy it, but in the end it's a job. I do it and when it's time to come home I'm more than ready.

Because I know Faith will be here.

Fuck me. I gave Gavin and Aden shit and here I am, more twisted around Faith than maybe even they are over their women.

And I don't give a damn.

That thought makes me grin. I check my watch and realize that Faith should be here any minute. I check the linguini one last time, satisfied it's good. Then I move the non-alcoholic champagne in the ice as I look at the table. That shit probably tastes like shit, but it was the best I could do. I want Faith to feel like everything is perfect.

I even got that crazy-ass aunt of Faith's to bring over some linens and it looks stylish even if I do say so myself. I'm relieved. With Ida Sue I wasn't sure what I'd end up with. I adjust the candles on the table for no other reason than I'm nervous and I want everything to be perfect. With one last look I walk into the bedroom, double checking on things in there. The rose petals are on the new sheets. Candles are all around. This seemed easy in my head, but now I have these thoughts planted there.

Should I light the candles now? Do I wait and break away to do it after dinner? What happens if she follows and sees what I'm doing before the surprise? If I light them now will I catch the damn house on fire?

I've turned into a damn chick. I shake my head and stalk back into the kitchen, just as Faith opens the door.

"Titan, I need to talk—" She stops talking once she turns around and sees me. Her eyes go to me, wearing the suit I wore when I got married to her in Vegas. She couldn't have missed that and probably it's playing my hand a little early, but it just seemed to feel right. I walk to the table and light the candles—silently kicking my ass because I should have lit those before she showed up. Then, I walk to her and take her bag from her, setting it on the table by the door. "What's this?" she asks, her voice breathless. I move behind her and help her out of her coat and hang it on the hook on the wall.

"I made my woman dinner," I whisper against her ear, placing a kiss against her pulse—which is jumping in her neck. Her body is tense and I'm starting to worry I've made a mistake here.

She tilts her head back to look at me, her blue eyes moving thoughtfully.

"What are you up to, Big Daddy?"

"I hope you're hungry," I tell her, kissing her forehead. I give her shoulders a squeeze before I move back around her, leading her to the table.

"I... let me go clean up first," she says, resisting my hold.

Damn it! Why didn't I think about that?

"You look gorgeous just like this," I argue, pulling out the chair for her to sit in.

"I look a mess. I've worked all day. Let me just go change."

"No! ... I mean, you look perfect, babe. Sit down and let me take care of you."

"Titan, you're wearing a fancy suit, for God's sake. I'm going to go freshen up," she says and takes off walking toward the bedroom.

"Faith, I really don't want—" I end with a groan, because it's too late and, short of grabbing her and forcing her to sit at the table, there's nothing I can do.

It's official. I suck in the romance department. I stand at the door when she walks into the bedroom.

"Titan," she gasps, looking around at the rose petals and all of the unlit candles.

I should have lit them.

"What's going on?" she asks, twirling around. I take the couple of steps it takes to get to her while reaching into my pants pocket. I go down on one knee, thinking at least I've managed to get this part right.

Faith's hands go to cover her mouth as she gasps again. Her body shakes and I get the feeling she's resisting the urge to jump up and down—at least I hope that's it and not her resisting running from the room. I hold out the ring box I took from my pocket and pop the top open, holding it up to her. Inside is her gold band from our wedding in Vegas—all cleaned and shined—and another ring covered in diamonds in a design the jeweler called a pear diamond design with a halo cut. I had no fucking clue what that was. I just know that it was pretty, it was loaded with diamonds and it looked good with Faith's band. I thought she would like it, but if she doesn't I'll take back and let her pick one out. I don't specifically care—I just want my ring on her hand.

"Faith Lucas Marsh, will you marry me?" I ask, making sure to put in my last name. We may have gone through with the annulment, but for a little bit she had my name and I want her to have it again. *I need it.*

"Oh my God."

"Want my ring on your finger, babe," I tell her.

"Oh my *God*!"

"I really fucking want to be able to call you my wife again," I grumble, refusing to get nervous because she hasn't said yes.

"Oh my *God*!!" she says again, adding even more of a squeal at the end. I'm thinking this is good news, but hell, who knows when it comes to a woman? She still hasn't said yes, though, so I decide to nudge her along.

"Faith? Is that a yes?"

"What?" she asks, confused, her gaze traveling back to my face —because it had been glued on the ring.

"Will you marry me?" I ask the question again, nervous because she's crying and women do cry when happy, but fuck, I'm a nervous wreck and I'm not sure which these are.

"Titan, I—" Fuck, she's going to turn me down. That definitely wasn't a yes.

"Faith—"

"Yes!!!!"

She screams the word and then lunges at me. I catch her, but I wasn't prepared so I fall back on my ass, my arms full of my woman, her arms around my neck, her face planted into my chest, her legs kicking happily and I don't think I've ever felt better. I hold her close and I do it laughing.

"I'll marry you. I'll marry you. *I'll marry you*!" she squeals over and over and that makes me laugh harder.

"Got the message, Faith. Can I put the ring on your hand?"

She pulls back and looks at me, settling into my lap so she's straddling me and more comfortable. I like it because even through our clothes I can feel her rub against me in all the right areas. I keep one hand on her hip, holding her steady and she holds out her hand, wiggling her fingers.

"Give me!" she demands and shit if that don't make me laugh

too. I take out the engagement ring and band together and slide it on her finger.

"I don't think I'm supposed to do the band again until we get in front of a preacher, but I want it back on your fucking finger now," I grumble, feeling emotions rushing through me that I've never let myself experience before. But, that's okay. I've got Faith and she's mine, and everything is new now.

"We have to go get you a ring! I want you to wear one too, Titan," she says staring down at her rings.

I bring my lips down to her hand and kiss just above her ring. Then I look at her and hold out my hand, showing I'm already wearing my band. That makes her tears fall harder and she hugs me close.

"I love you, Titan," she whispers. Those words wrap inside of me, around and around my heart in a way that's both painful and full of joy and even peace at the same time. I want to give her the words back, but I hold back. Not because I don't feel them, but because before I can she pulls away and looks at me and says something that leaves me speechless.

"Hope says we need to have a hooker pirate wedding."

I don't say anything. Honestly, I think it takes a bit for my mind to understand what she said and even when I do, I'm not sure I know *what* it means. It doesn't matter, though, because in the next minute, Faith's lips are on mine, my tongue is in her mouth and her hips are grinding down on me. That's my cue so I make love to my soon to be wife and I do it not giving a fuck about the unlit candles.

52

FAITH

"Titan? Are you awake?" I ask. I keep my voice quiet, just in case he is sleeping.

The room is dark. Sometime between the second time we made love, enjoyed a warmed-up dinner and lit the candles in the bedroom, before going another round, which included Titan using his mouth on me, and then taking me from behind, after which I used my mouth on him—the candles had long since burned out. Marathon lovemaking was something I had never experienced, didn't know was possible, but definitely want to repeat again.

The room is pretty dark now, except for the light of the moon shining through the double windows. I'm wrapped in Titan's arms, my head on his chest and my ear pressed down so I can hear the steady beat of his heart.

My body is relaxed, sated, and sore in all the right spots. When Titan doesn't answer right away I figure he must be asleep and I squeeze him a little tighter and burrow deeper into his body heat.

"I'm awake," he whispers, and I feel him kiss the top of my head, which makes me smile. "You wore me out, so I'm spent. So, if you want my dick, you're out of luck. With a little encouragement, I might can give you my mouth again, but you better hurry because I'm wiped," he mumbles, making me grin.

"Your dick is safe."

"Thank God for that."

"At least for now," I giggle when he groans. He gives me a squeeze and it's sweet and I close my eyes as that sweetness hits me.

"What's on your mind, wife?" he asks and the sweetness in that word is even better.

Spectacular even.

"I don't want a pirate wedding," I tell him, having told him Hope's idea over dinner.

"Anything you want, you get."

"You don't care?"

"As long as it ends up with your last name Marsh, you waking up in my bed and not running halfway across the world, I'm good."

"Good to know." I grin, biting down on my lip. Titan's hand is brushing on my thigh and it feels divine.

"That all before I pass out because my woman just wore my dick out?"

Again another giggle surges up. I sure hope you can't die from happiness because if you can—*I might be in trouble.*

"I know what kind of wedding I want."

"Anything you want, Faith, because this will be your last one."

That was a different kind of sweet, but I liked it more.

"Since this will be the only wedding you get too, don't you want a say in it? What about your family?"

"Not close with any of them."

"Not close with any of them?" I ask, not liking that for him. I didn't have much family I could count on, but I was thankful for the ones that I did have.

"Money changes things and for a time I had plenty of it. I paid that forward. My fam needed something, I gave. I felt the urge to be gifty, I gave more. Soon, my giving and their needs became more about their wants, and less about being family. Less about gratitude. When the money began to slow, their presence in my life did too."

"That's kind of sad."

"It is. It's also life. So you plan your wedding and make it about what you want. I don't care as long as in the end you're with me."

"I want to give you a wedding you like, Titan," I murmur, my mind working in a million directions.

"You are."

"How do you know that?"

"I get you. You're taking my name and you're giving me a baby. I'm good, Faith. I swear it to you. I'm more than good," he says and his hand goes to my stomach, holding it, and that warms me all the way through.

"I want to get married at my aunt's home. Surrounded by my family and whoever you want there. I want this wedding to be one we have pictures of, show our child and have them know they belong, that they have love."

Titan goes still and I twist so I can look up at him. He's staring down at me and his face is shaded in the darkness, so I can't see what's going on. I start to ask, but a second later his hand comes up to slide under my hair and gently hold me on the side of my neck. His thumb brushes the corner of my lip and he ever so slowly brings our lips together.

"We'll give them all of that," he mumbles before sealing that promise in a kiss. When we break apart he moves me back into his body and I hold him close again. "We'll give them all of that, even if I have a bruised ass from your loco-aunt pinching it all day."

I giggle again, because I can picture that in my head.

"I'll have a word with her," I promise.

"It won't do any good," he counters and he's right.

"You're right," I confirm out loud.

"Now can we get some sleep so my dick can recover and I can get lost inside of you again?"

"Well... uh..."

"Faith?"

"You mentioned giving me your mouth?" I question greedily.

His body goes stiff under me again, and I bite my lip again. Then he moves us so I'm on my back against the bed and his fingers are already seeking between my legs.

"You're wet," he groans.

"You're naked in bed with me," I answer, because that's all it takes and most of the time it takes a lot less than that. Titan's that lethal. I let my fingers slide through his hair, teasing my fingertips.

"Changed my mind," he growls, shifting so he's over me, looking down, his weight on his arms.

"What do you mean?" I ask, distracted because in this position I can drag my nails down his chest.

"Want my dick inside of you."

"You can handle another round?" I ask. I grin, because I know he can, because I feel his cock brushing against me.

"It's a miracle," he growls, positioning himself at my center. "Give me your mouth, Faith," he growls as he sinks inside of me.

I lean up and give Titan my mouth as I take him into my body.

And that's a different kind of sweet than any I've had tonight. It's heaven. As my eyes open I look up into the eyes of the man I love and my rings are shining in the darkness.

That's when I know.

You can't die from too much happiness, because I'm overfilled with it and my heart is beating strong.

53

TITAN

"You sure about this, man?" Aden asks and I look over at him and Gavin and I do it with a smile firmly in place.

"Never more fucking sure in my life," I tell them and that's when they nod in approval and slap me on the back. The three of us turn to face the crowd as the music starts.

We're in the backyard of Ida Sue's house. There's flowers and roll of white satin on the ground. Two rows of chairs surround the white satin aisle and they're filled to capacity. All with Faith's family. Other than Gavin and Aden, I had no one I wanted to invite. They were who was important in my life and that's all I need.

I watch as two little boys walk up the aisle carrying a sign. The signs are wooden and painted brown, with calligraphy writing on them. One is Hope and Aden's boy, Jack, and the other is Luka and Petal's little boy River. The sign they are packing says: "Happily Ever After Coming Soon." Behind them there is another boy, older, though not that old, and he is clearly a Lucas, though I have no idea whose. He keeps looking over at Green as if to say *I don't want to be here*—so I'd say his if I was to venture a guess. His sign proclaims, "Last Chance To Run" in the same writing. I shake my head, figuring Ida Sue had something to do with this. The crowd laughs quietly, but loud enough you can hear it over the music playing in the background over outdoor speakers.

Next comes Petal, wearing an off-white dress with a bright yellow silk bow at the waist. The bow is in the back, but clearly visible at her hips. She looks beautiful, despite looking like she is about to pop. She comes down the aisle, smiling over at her husband Luka. He winks at her and she stops for a minute and looks at him.

"Quit going all moon-eyed over Orange. You've been married forever. Can't you tell my Chocolate Thunder wants his bride!" Ida Sue chastises. I hold my head down, pinching the bridge of my nose while everyone around us laughs—loudly.

"Looks like I need to show you who you belong to again, Lovey," Jansen grumbles, and I look up to see the man shoot me a look meant to kill. I shake my head.

"I cleaned the playhouse earlier this morning," she says, patting his leg, and I don't think I want to know what that means.

Faith's family is whacked.

Next comes Casey. She is dressed in the same kind of off-white dress, bright yellow silk bow at the waist. They met during the last two weeks—because that was how long it took Faith to get this wedding together. She wanted months—as in after the baby was born. I refused. I wanted my ring legally on her finger and my name legally recorded. This was something I wouldn't budge on. She respected it and called in Hope for reinforcements. Her sister Charity wasn't reachable, which bummed Faith out, but she didn't ask me to postpone the wedding again and I was thankful—because for that I would have.

Faith and Casey hit it off when Hope brought her down to help plan the wedding. They got along so well that Faith asked Casey to be part of the wedding. I liked it. I like that my wife bonded with my best friend's wives. Because Gavin and Aden are as close to brothers as I will ever have. They're my family and Faith understands that.

The music changes timbre every so slight and then Hope walks down the aisle. She's wearing the same type of dress but the style is a bit different. And, where Petal and Casey have yellow daisies, Hope has a bouquet of white ones with yellow centers. She walks up slowly, her eyes completely on Aden. I look at my brother and he doesn't take his eyes from her either, even as she goes and stands in her place.

The music shifts again and this isn't a wedding march. I know this song. It's not one I'd listen to freely and pick of my own, but I like the words. I like what they say and I like that Faith picked them.

A woman begins singing about how her doubt goes away and as she sings out about being one step closer, Faith comes into view.

With each step, the lyrics of the song is driven closer. They're not wrong. I was dying and waiting for Faith even if I didn't realize it. I was making jacked-up decisions before the blond tornado stormed into my life, taking it over.

"Damn, boys, we did good," Gavin says and he's not wrong. He's one hundred percent not wrong.

Faith makes it to me right as the woman sings about loving her man for a thousand years. Her gaze holds mine. She's in a beautiful crystal white dress, and she gives Hope her solid white bouquet wrapped with a yellow bow and then turns to me.

"I'll love you for a thousand more," she whispers as I bend down to kiss her and the music softly ends.

"I'll love you longer, wife," I whisper as we break apart and tears slide from her eyes. "You ready to do this for real this time?"

"More than ready," she whispers.

"Stop!" someone shouts from the area Faith just marched from. I growl and turn around to see a dude with blond hair, wearing maroon corduroy pants and a gray pullover sweater walking toward us. He looks familiar but I'm too filled with the urge to choke him to latch onto why.

"Oh my God," Faith growls, her voice angry.

"Who is that asshole?"

"That's Brad," she hisses.

That's when I remember the picture of him and Faith together.

"Faith, you can't marry this man. You're meant to be with me," he says.

"Damn it, Black! I thought you and Blue were supposed to make sure the gates were locked so vermin couldn't get in," Ida Sue yells, getting out of her seat in the front row and walking to us.

"Brad, what in the hell are you doing here?"

"I'm here to stop you from the biggest mistake you'll ever make. You can't love this man, Faith. You're mine. You were always meant to be mine," he says and he's stupid as all fuck, but he has to have balls, I'll give him that. But this is my wedding. I want it done and he's already messed part of Faith's dream wedding up and I've had it. I turn so that Faith is behind me and face him.

"That's where you're wrong. She was yours and you pissed that away because you're a stupid fuck. She's mine now and, like I told you before, I'm not a stupid fuck. I'm not letting her go."

"Mommy, what's fuck?" I hear River asking in the background, but I ignore it.

"I'll tell you later," Petal mumbles.

"Like in twenty years," Luka says, coming to stand by Ida Sue.

"You also said you were married to Faith, and clearly you're not. So you don't factor into this," he says, acting like he's a freaking king talking to a lonely peasant. "Faith, let's just go. We'll put this behind us. I can forgive you for wanting to walk on the wild side and lowering yourself to..."

"What are you even saying?" Faith asks, her anger rising, mostly because I think she understands what he's insinuating. Dealt with this bullshit all my life and it is bullshit. I want to introduce him to my fist, but I'm holding back because I don't want to ruin my girl's wedding, when he opens his mouth again.

"I'm saying that you wanted to experiment and I get it, but you can't seriously mean to tie yourself to him. He's beneath you."

"In what way?" Faith asks and I know that look my woman has.

"He's not..." The man fumbles for words, no doubt trying to

come up with something that doesn't make him sound like the racist bastard he is. "You're just not one of *our* kind. No offense meant. I give to the negro college fund all the time," he says and I snort in laughter.

"No offense taken, man. I'm skipping for joy inside that I'm not like you," I laugh.

"Well, I'm offended," Faith growls and she reaches down and takes the sign that River was helping to carry and then she does something I figured was coming, but still makes me laugh. She hits old Brad up the side of the head.

She doesn't do it lightly, and that's evidenced when Brad goes down. Dumbass doesn't stay down, though, and once he gets back up, he's fuming.

"You bitch!" he growls. I put Faith back behind me and I'm getting ready to lay out the bastard. I don't get the chance, though, because before I can, Ida Sue lets out an eardrum-splitting whistle.

"Hamburger!" she yells. "Time to take out the trash." Then she mutters a little quieter—but not that quiet, "Ruining my Chocolate Thunder's beautiful day. Not to mention Blossom's. I ought to do worse." And then, no joke, this cow comes lumbering toward us. He stops in front of Ida Sue and she pets him and then points at Brad. "Get rid of him," she orders.

I thought she was insane. I thought I was seeing things. Maybe I am, and definitely she probably is, but that damn cow bites Brad on the ass. He screams like a little girl, holding his ass, but the cow does it again and this time he comes away with a piece of corduroy on his mouth which he—or she, I don't really hang with cows—begins chewing on.

"I demand you—" Brad starts, to which the cow bites him again. I blink, but the image doesn't go away. Brad's walking away, and even starting to move fast because every minute or so the cow is biting him. Pretty soon old Brad takes off running with Ida Sue's pet cow on his heels. It's the strangest fucking thing I've ever seen. Everyone is laughing, but my eyes are still glued to the disappearing cow when I feel Faith tug on my arm.

"Let's get married, Big Daddy," she laughs. I jump, then look behind me because Ida Sue just pinched me on the ass. I look up at the sky wondering exactly what I'm getting myself into. "I love you, Titan," Faith says and I look back at her, still shaking my head.

It doesn't matter how crazy her family is. They're a good kind of crazy and my woman loves me, so that's okay. I do hope our child doesn't take after Ida Sue, however.

And you can't blame a man for that.

54

FAITH

"What are you thinking, Big Daddy?" I ask Titan. The wedding has been over for a while now. We've cut the cake and enjoyed the reception. Aunt Ida Sue even managed to wrangle her cow, Hamburger, back up. Despite Brad's appearance, it's been a great day.

"That white people are crazy," he mumbles and then I look up in surprise. We're dancing together, music playing in the background and the sun is starting to fade in the sky, leaving a beautiful mixture of pink, orange, blue and purples in its wake. I follow his line of sight and watch as Petal and Luka leave the playhouse.

"Um—"

"That's the third couple that's gone in there today, Faith."

"Um—"

"And I'm pretty sure they're not measuring the windows for drapes," he says and I can't stop the giggle that escapes.

"Our kids will never play in that playhouse, wife."

"Ida Sue keeps it clean," I answer encouragingly.

"Never playing in that damn playhouse," he grumbles.

"Point made, but if you're going to draw the line there, you might not want them eating at the kitchen table."

"Christ."

"Or in the barn…"

"Jesus," he mutters.

"Or on the front porch swing. There's even this one spot on the roof—"

"Which brings me back to my point. White people are fucking *whacked*," he mutters.

I loop my hands up around his neck, our bodies close and still swaying to the music.

"I had a perfect wedding," I whisper and he brings his dark eyes back to me.

"Until your ex showed up and decided to mess it up."

"That's almost my favorite part."

"Say what?"

"I'll never get the vision of Hamburger biting into Brad's ass out of my head. It was *hilarious*!" I tell him, dragging out the word and putting emphasis on the "us" part.

"I doubt old Brad will forget it either, since he probably has cow teeth scars on his ass."

"Which is awesome," I giggle and Titan shakes his head at me.

"I'm starting to think my wife is whacked," he mutters.

"But you love me," I whisper and he brings his mouth down to mine.

"That I do, wife. That I do," he grins, kissing me softly.

"And you want me happy," I tell him.

"Definitely want my woman happy," he agrees, and he says it so earnestly I squeeze him tighter.

"You'd give me anything I want, really," I murmur, letting my fingers move down his neck and around to the sides.

"What are you playing at, wife?" Titan asks, his voice skeptical.

"Well, I'm pregnant and sometimes we have weird… *cravings*," I hedge, trying to remain looking innocent as he watches me closely.

"You want pickles and ice cream?" he asks.

"Ew, no."

"Thank God."

"But I do want something..."

"What is it? If I can get it for you, I will."

"See, you are so sweet."

"That's me. My wife owns my balls, so what do you want?"

"You to take me into the playhouse," I grin.

"Um... fuck no."

"But you have to, Titan."

"Hell no, I don't. Did you not hear me when I told you that's the third couple today that's gone in there?"

"Well, yeah, but..."

"My dick will not be going where three other dicks have been in one damn day," he mumbles and I can see this is going to be a hard sale.

"Good to know," I answer, trying to hold back a laugh.

"You want fucked, I'll take you home and fuck you."

"So romantic," I mutter.

"You want romance, then I'll turn music on while I fuck you."

"I think you're missing the point. It's a family tradition."

"Say what?"

"Playing house in the playhouse as it were. It's a family tradition," I explain patiently.

"You're shitting me," he says, clearly not convinced.

"Nope, and every married couple who's had a taste of their honeymoon in that old playhouse is still happily married years later."

"Faith—"

"With lots of kids."

"Faith—"

"I want to be married to you forever, Titan."

"Damn it, Faith," he groans.

"And it should be said that I definitely want more kids."

"Christ."

"And it should also be noted that your dick won't be going in the playhouse as it were. It will be going in me."

Titan doesn't answer, but he picks me up and starts stomping toward the playhouse, so I'm thinking that's answer enough.

EPILOGUE

Titan

I look down at my sleeping bride. We aren't doing a honeymoon, though we both plan on it. It's just we both started new jobs and there was no way to get the time off right now. Still, we're married and she has my last name, and that makes today perfect—even with her damn ex showing up. I turn and go through the house, making sure the doors are locked and then start turning out the lights. I stop in the small room off the master that Faith has been decorating for the nursery. She chose a yellow, which seems to be her favorite color and works since it's not a color for just a girl or a boy. It's bare right now, the walls painted a creamy pale yellow and the carpet a neutral soft mushroom. We're going next week to pick out furniture for the room and Faith mentioned decorating it in flowers. I'm fine with the idea, but there will be no daughters named after flowers, or boys named after colors like her aunt did. She's promised that the whole Zeus thing was off the table too.

Which is good. My child needs a normal name, one that says she'll be calm and not run her father around in circles, making him dizzy.

I walk back into our bedroom, pulling off my pajama bottoms. I don't wear pajamas, but Faith bought these. She told me she didn't want me swinging my dick around the house and Ida Sue showing up unexpectedly. I started to argue until she pointed out if her aunt got one look at what I was packing she would never leave me alone.

"Faith, you're being—"

"I'm a woman, Titan and trust me when I tell you, Big Daddy. If any woman sees what you're packing, she's going to start following you around like a little lost puppy dog."

I wanted to argue, but when a woman has that much pride in your dick the wise move is to let it go. So I wear the pajamas around the house, but never to bed. I never let Faith wear shit to bed either. I wanted her naked. I wanted her naked against me and when I want to touch her, I sure as hell don't want clothes between us. Luckily, Faith agreed completely with this rule.

As I slide into bed beside her, she burrows into me and I take a deep, satisfied breath. Our relationship may have started off in all the wrong ways. She may have pulled me from my normal, calm life and forced me to chase her down, but I don't mind. Faith is the best thing that ever happened to me. She's everything and I'd do it all again, relive every crazy moment and the only thing I would have changed is that I would have chased her harder and faster.

"Titan," she murmurs in her sleep, snuggling into me, and I smile as I pull her in closer.

My eyes close and I drift to sleep thinking I am a man who has a miracle in his arms. Later I dream of a small little girl with beautiful blue eyes the color of the ocean, skin a golden brown, and the perfect mixture of me and her mother. I dream of that beautiful face, knowing God has given me a glimpse of my future and I do it smiling. Maybe calm is overrated. Chaos might be good.

Eris Sue Marsh was born seven months later at 2:00 a.m. in the morning. She arrived in the middle of a torrential rain that sparked tornados and flooding. Inside the hospital all was quiet, though, and her parents had to admit they had a piece of perfection even in the chaos.

THE END

Turn the page for a sneak peek of my book, Devil, Savage Brothers—Tennessee Chapter, coming your way very soon and up for preorder.

PROLOGUE

Devil

I've heard most of my life, that a man doesn't let his dick lead him. I don't know who the fuck came up with that, but it sounds like a boring life. Leading with my dick has led me to some of the sweetest pussy a man could hope to touch and, quite simply, I'm a man who likes to fuck. I'm also a man, not a boy. I'm almost thirty-six years old and I live my life exactly like I want. I don't have bullshit that holds me back from what I want.

I take what I want.

Sanctimonious assholes can look down on me and how I choose to live my life, they won't be the first and they probably won't be the last. While they're doing that I'm usually swimming with pussy in my bed. That's my life and I make no apologies. The woman—or women—know the score before they climb in the bed and join the party. They get what they want and I get what I want. It's a beautiful bargain. The only loyalty I have is to my club.

Until her.

I used to look at bastards like my Vice President Crusher and just stop and wonder what in the world could be so special about one pussy that his dick would get so wound up it'd be willing to give up other women. That kind of bullshit confused the hell out of me. The thought of just having one woman for the rest of my life terrified me *and* my dick.

Until her.

One look at her and it was like I was struck by lightning. Sounds like a fucking cliché, but it's true all the same.

I'm standing in the pharmacy aisle at the local K-Mart stocking up on condoms. I might like sticking my cock in a lot of different holes, but I do that shit smart. One, I'm partial to my dick and I'm not sticking it in any snatch where when I pull out it's going to come out looking like it's been stuck into a beehive. Women can look smoking hot on the outside, their pussy can smell like fucking lilacs in the spring—but inside it can be deadly. I will never be caught without a condom and that's the fucking truth.

I usually order the damn things in bulk, but there's been hurricanes everywhere and I'm not risking my dick because of a delayed shipment.

I wheel my cart around—only having a cart because I'm a lazy ass motherfucker who wants to lean on it, but also because the boss told me to pick up some beer and shit for the club. Other chapters have open bars and crap. Our group is smaller. There's a room, there's a fucking wall of refrigerators and a bar where the alcohol goes. There's no bartender and we stock that shit ourselves. We're trying to convince our Prez, Diesel, to get the prospects to do that shit. But the bastard has been dealing with people trying to steal his kid since from day one almost, and he's very picky about who he trusts. Prospects for the club have guarded access at best until they prove themselves and there's very fucking few of those. I can't say as I blame him.

My usual brand of condom is the "Legend." I don't mean to brag but fuck, the name fits my cock and it's made for big and wide, both of which—thank God—is me. If I was one of these poor bastards born with a pencil dick I probably would have swallowed a bullet by now. Some men can deal with that blow from mother nature—hell, maybe they even compensate by learning to use their tongue to bag their women, fuck if I know. I just know I'm *not* one of those men. I love my dick and it works out well the women do too.

They don't sell Legends at K-Mart, and that sucks. I find the extra-large, ribbed for her pleasure and extra strength latex and grab those. I throw about ten boxes in the buggy and slide down until they lean against the three cartons of beer.

"Planning a party?" a soft voice asks me and that's the moment it happens. The moment my dick gets so tangled up in a woman the bastard will never get free—which sucks, because my dick and I are attached.

She's beautiful. A brunette with long, silky hair and eyes the shade of whiskey. Her skin is a golden tan and so smooth I ache to touch it just looking at her. She's dressed in a white skirt that hugs her curves—and she's got a lot of them—and falls just at the edge of the prettiest knees I've ever seen. Her legs don't have stockings on, it's just them and they're as golden as the rest of her. A woman who lays out in the sun and lets the rays worship her body. That's the image that comes to mind and I fight down the urge to adjust myself—evidence my dick has the same image.

"I was, until I saw you. Do you like parties, Angel?"

She's standing with her back to me, but her head turned to capture my gaze. Her eyes blink at my pet name. Her body stiffens, but that could be because my eyes are still glued to her ass and the way it stretches the material of her skirt.

When she turns to face me, I finally drag my gaze back to her top, which is just as good. She's wearing a soft pink top with a high collar that doesn't give me a chance to see her cleavage—and that makes me damn sad. Still, it hugs her tits and those are nice and big. A man could bury his face in them if he felt the urge to go motor boating and he could bury his dick in them if he wanted to go face surfing.

The best of both worlds.

"I have a feeling I'm not really into your type of parties," she says, her voice a mixture of laughter and sweetness. It's a damn good voice, perfect and goes with the rest of her.

Damn.

"What's your name?"

"Does it matter?"

"My heart will wither up and die without it," I answer, making her laugh, those beautiful pink-glossed lips of hers spreading in a smile.

I can't stop myself from letting my eyes travel up and down her body one more time. She's got these white shoes on with a wide heel, her toes peeking out of them.

I'll fuck her while she's wearing nothing but those shoes.

"I think you might be lying to me," she murmurs.

"You ready to roll, man? Diesel will have our asses if we don't get back," Drummer says, rounding the aisle that me and my dream woman are standing in.

"In a bit," I tell him, not taking my eyes away from her.

She looks at Drummer, though. I frown because that's the moment I know I'm in *real* trouble.

For the first time in my life I feel jealousy.

Drummer has no trouble getting women. He doesn't get as much pussy as I do, but only because he doesn't try. Women tend to flock to him, digging the bad boy vibe mixed with the blond hair and blue eyes look that could have him mistaken for the boy next door.

She turns back to look at me, her eyes finding mine, and the look on her face is thoughtful.

"Enjoy your party, boys," she says softly, and then starts to move around the corner. I reach out and grab her arm. I instantly love it, and curse myself for it.

Electricity and heat shoot through me like a bolt of lightning. It hasn't happened before. I've never felt anything like it, but it's there. I think she feels it too, because she jerks in my hold. Or fuck, maybe she's just unnerved a man she doesn't know is putting hands on her. Couldn't blame her for that and I've never done something like this in my life—but I don't let her go.

"How about I let Drummer take the shit back and I take you out for a drink instead?"

She swallows. I know because I'm watching her that closely. She rubs her lips together, spreading the gloss on them even more, and I feel the exact moment a shiver runs through her body. She's not immune to me, or I'm freaking her out. That seems fair, since my reaction to her is doing the same to me.

"What about your party?"

"You and I can have our own party," I tell her easily and I hear Drummer mumble in the background, but I tune him out.

"I don't think I'm the kind of girl who goes to your parties," she laughs.

"Devil, come on. We got to get a move on," Drummer growls and swear to God I'm going to junk-punch his whiney ass for sounding like a harping girlfriend.

"Devil?" she asks, and I grin.

"That's my road name, Angel."

"Angel? Devil? That's kind of lame, isn't it?"

"I think it's more like fate," I answer, loving the way she's relaxed into my hold.

"I'm not your angel. Trust me on that one," she laughs.

"Are you ready, Sister Tori?" Another woman comes around the corner, looking at my Angel.

"In a minute," she says.

"Is there a problem, gentlemen?" the other girl says. I give her a glance. She's passably pretty. She's wearing a longer skirt, and a shirt that is buttoned to the neck. Her hair is in a bun and she's showing no skin except her face and hands. On some women you'd get the urge to undo the hair and see what's she's hiding under those clothes. This woman doesn't give you that urge. This woman makes me feel like one look and she could cause my balls to go into permanent hiding. It's unsettling, to say the least.

"No problem, I was just asking... Tori? Is that your name, Angel?"

"It's short for Torrent," she supplies helpfully, taking her arm out of my hold. I let her go, but I sure as hell don't want to.

"Torrent... I like that. I like that a lot."

"My life is more complete, then," she jokes.

"Tori, Mother Lisa will be waiting for us," the other woman says.

Something is nudging into my brain—which is mostly fogged by the beautiful woman in front of me.

"Mother Lisa? Kind of a strange way to refer to your mom, isn't it?" I question, my eyes never leaving Torrent's.

"It's not when she's the Superior."

"The Superior?" I ask. Not quite getting it.

"As in Mother Superior." She smiles, and that smile is a little too sweet.

"I—"

"Oh shit. You two are nuns?" Drummer asks. My body stiffens and I jerk as if I've been punched in the gut—because I have.

"Told you I wasn't the girl for your parties," she says. "I'm ready," she says turning back to her friend. "You gentlemen have a good evening. I'll say some prayers for you... *Devil*," she adds and then, just like that she leaves me standing with a cart full of condoms and not an urge one to use them tonight.

Damn it.

Preorder at your favorite retailer today!

Preorder Devil Here!

READ MORE JORDAN

With These Titles:

Doing Bad Things Series

Going Down Hard (Free On All Markets)
In Too Deep
Taking It Slow

Savage Brothers MC—TN Chapter

Devil

Savage Brothers MC

Breaking Dragon
Saving Dancer
Loving Nicole
Claiming Crusher
Trusting Bull
Needing Carrie

Devil's Blaze MC

Captured
Craved
Burned
Released
Shafted
Beast
Beauty

Lucas Brothers Series

Perfect Stroke
Raging Heart On
Happy Trail

Filthy Florida Alphas Series

Unlawful Seizure
Unjustified Demands
Unwritten Rules

LINKS:

Here's my social media links! Make sure you sign up for my newsletter. I give things away there and you get to see things before others! I also have a blog on my webpage you can subscribe to and besides my strange ramblings I'll update you on my work in progress.

Newsletter Subscription
Facebook Page
Twitter
Webpage
Bookbub
Instagram
Text Alerts: (US only)
Text JORDAN to 797979
Standard Text Messaging Rates May Apply

Made in the USA
Columbia, SC
20 January 2021

31299187R00128